Masquerade

Donna Campbell

Donna Campbell

Edited by Jim Barringer
Of
Barringer Books
www.thinkaboutfaith.com
www.facebook.com/BarringerBooks

Published by DC Books
Ocoee, FL
www.DonnaLCampbell.com

Cover models Vanessa Giorgi and Harry Rubi

No part of this book may be reproduced or transmitted in any form or by any means without permission in writing from the publisher.

Copyright © 2016 Donna Campbell
All rights reserved.
ISBN: 153706861X
ISBN-13: 978-1537068619

DEDICATION

This book is dedicated to my readers. Those of you who take the time to read the story that poured out of my brain and fingers. I am overwhelmed that anyone would be interested in the thoughts, ideas, and yarns that I write. I write them because I must. I publish them because you ask me to do that.
I love all five of you! ;-)

ACKNOWLEDGMENTS

There are so many people to thank. I want to thank the people like Liz, Rich, and Emely who contributed real stories of hardship, relationship difficulties, and forgiveness so that I could include them in Deborah's story. I want to thank certain singers (Josh Brown, Matt Carter, Toby Morrell) who noticed me in the crowd and chose to remember me and then befriend me. You as well as many other friends helped me learn I am just as worth knowing as you are.

Thank you Lani, Angie, and Rachel for your input and encouragement.

It may be unusual to thank an editor in the acknowledgments, but I was so impressed with Jim and Andrea Barringer of Barringer Books and ThinkaboutFaith.com for the excellent job of editing this novel. The care you took with her meant a great deal. I look forward to entrusting my next book to you.

Dance Card

Part One 1
Prologue 2
Mansion on a Hill 4
Home 10
Good Rockin' Tonight 14
Dirty Little Secret 19
Boys Keep Swinging 29
Roam 35
New York 40
The Sound of Music 42
The Good Life 45
I Will Remember You 47
Holiday 52
Lost Boy 54
Don't Judge Me 58
Two Princes 62
Lost in Paradise 66
Secrets 71
Fancy 76
Walkin' on Sunshine 81
Life Love and Hope 85
Nowhere Man 89
Reapers Dance 95
Why Can't We be Friends 101
Luka 106
RearViewMirror 110

Masquerade

At Least That's What You Said	115
Not Yet	118
Christmas is Coming	121
Feelings	124
Winter Wonderland	127
Cold	132
I Want to Tell You	138
Baby, It's Cold Outside	143
Mayfly	147
The Masquerade Ball	151
9:00	152
10:00	156
11:00	160
Midnight	164
Part Two	167
Broken	168
Trick Me	176
Starting Over	181
Question	187
Brand New Sun	194
You're So Vain	200
Me Time	206
Beautiful Goodbye	210
You'll Never Walk Alone	214
Letting Go	218
Amazing Grace	223
The Heart of the Matter	227
Turn Turn Turn	231
Brand New Day	238

Plan on Forever	243
Take Me Home Country Roads	247
With a Little Help From My Friends	251
Going Home	254
I Hope	258
Homeward Bound	261
We Are Family	268
Less Than Whole	273
The Wedding	279
Wedding Day	280
One Hand One Heart	285
One Soul	290
Epilogue	295

PART ONE

PROLOGUE

Deborah Wade was seventeen years old and held the hope of her future in her hand: her acceptance letter to Quinnipiac University in Connecticut, over a thousand miles from the backyard birthday party at her parents' house in Florida. Already dreaming of a future when she would throw a party like this for her children, surrounding them with the love of a family, the joy of friends, and the security of people who cared about them, she scanned the crowd for her parents so she could share the good news.

The summer sun warmed Deborah's face as she made her way past the hot dog and hamburger buffet, in front of the rented bounce house, and through the middle of the kids' game of keep-away. She couldn't find her parents anywhere in the sea of people. Finally, Deborah caught sight of her dad with the birthday girl, six-year-old Daisy Rodriguez. She watched her father lead Daisy by the hand back into the house.

Deborah trotted after them into the kitchen, eager to show off the letter, but didn't see her dad or Daisy. Where could they have disappeared to? At last, she heard her dad's voice coming from the laundry room. "I have a special gift just for you, sweetie." She opened the door to the laundry room to see his large hand over the girl's small one, placing it on his naked groin.

For an instant time froze. She was suddenly three years old again, as long-buried memories and images invaded her mind. Everything felt disconnected, as if she were watching a movie from far away. Then terror mixed with nausea overwhelmed Deborah and brought her back to the present, to reality. A strangled cry of "Stop!" leaped out of her throat. She grabbed the tiny and frightened child and swept her out into the empty living room.

Daisy was crying by then, and as Deborah tried to soothe her, she realized she too was crying. She stood clinging to Daisy for several minutes, unable to think of anything but the child's safety, before resolving to find Daisy's parents. Carrying the girl to the doorway that led from the kitchen to the yard, she caught the eye of Daisy's mother. Whatever Lacy Rodriguez saw in Deborah's face, it made her grab her husband Jose and rush into the kitchen.

Lacy reached out for her daughter. Deborah found it difficult to let go, but she came to her senses and reluctantly relinquished the child. "What happened? My Lord! Is Daisy okay? Are you? What happened?" Her voice grew increasingly panicked and Daisy's sobs became louder. Lacy forced herself to sound calm and tried to soothe her weeping child, listening in horror as Deborah told her everything.

Donna Campbell

MANSION ON A HILL

Deborah was surrounded by opulence but none of it was hers. She was the personal secretary to Mrs. Arthur Copeland, a wealthy widow, socialite, and philanthropist. Catherine Copeland's home was a palatial mansion on a bucolic estate which made the mansions near it look like bungalows in comparison. It even had a name, Cumberland Manor, though most people referred to it as Cumberland. A person could address their mail to Cumberland Manor, Belle Cay, Connecticut, and the letter would come to the right place without the street name or number. Catherine Copeland ruled her home as if she carried the title of duchess, and Deborah had often thought that she may as well be one. The rest of those who called themselves high society treated her as royalty, and she was happy to oblige them.

That spring morning, the two sat on the balcony patio which overlooked the swimming pool below and the strolling garden beyond the pool. Deborah was taking notes for an upcoming auction, which would raise money for the Arthur Copeland Foundation. Catherine Copeland had not been born in

England, but she affected a slight British accent when she spoke.

"Miss Wade, order the invitations from Boothby's by tomorrow so that I can see the proof by Tuesday next. You have the list. Ensure that you include William Jefferies and his new bride. I've forgotten her name. He married his assistant." Catherine leaned in closer to her assistant and lowered her voice. "She got that job only so she could catch a rich husband. The man thought he was in love and he refused a prenuptial. I believe he thought she would refuse to sign it and he would lose her. He doesn't have the looks or personality to attract a wife; I suppose his money is the only thing that could get him one."

Deborah paused her writing, waiting for Mrs. Copeland to finish her monologue and return to business. The woman's speech was peppered with frequent criticism and opinions when the two of them were together, or when she was in the company of just a few women. It didn't matter to her that most of her sentiments were insulting to Deborah. To Mrs. Copeland, money and pedigree mattered, and Deborah had neither. At last the lady of the house returned to planning the auction. Deborah was released to her small office, which was located next to Mrs. Copeland's own well-appointed one, to complete that day's responsibilities.

Deborah liked her job; Mrs. Copeland was not difficult to work for, even despite her snobbish attitude. Underneath the self-importance was a kind of noble benevolence. Deborah was kept very busy, but her work was often interesting, and she was paid well enough. She had come to work for Mrs. Copeland six months before, and found she had a knack for planning and administration. She was able to maintain an attitude of respect, civility, and privacy that Mrs. Copeland required. Too often she was her employer's confidant, but rather than disapprove of the woman or criticize her for her gossip, she tried to be compassionate. Deborah was not aware that she might have heard more in her employer's words than were there.

She sketched out a preliminary invitation, called Mr. Boothby to arrange a meeting, and then began working on Oliver Copeland's household finances. This was one part of her job she didn't completely understand. Oliver Copeland was the eldest Copeland son. He was married, had a child of his own, and held the top position in his late father's company, Copeland Enterprises. Yet instead of his wife or even his accountant being entrusted with his domestic affairs, it was Deborah's job to arrange the household payroll and budget.

Oliver was by far the kindest of the Copelands; he was said to take after his father, whom Deborah had never met because he had died five years before. Oliver had been in a skiing accident about two years earlier, which left him with a limp and some weakness. He had not returned to his position at the company yet and only held it in title at present. It seemed to Deborah he was somewhat coddled by his mother. In theory, the accident was the reason Deborah handled his house staff payroll, but she often wondered why it was not Kelly Copeland's job, since she was Oliver's wife. Why would an accident two years earlier stop the man from taking care of his own budget? She supposed it was his mother's way of cossetting a son she viewed as weak.

Oliver was certainly a meek man, but Deborah didn't see him as entirely weak, except in relation to his wife. Mrs. Copeland always had plenty to say about her daughter in law. When she informed Deborah about this part of her job, she berated Kelly in a lengthy soliloquy. "She would have divorced Oliver after his accident if she could, but I made her sign a prenuptial agreement and she was not willing to give up his money for her freedom." She clicked her tongue, took a sip of coffee and continued, "Oh no! She needs her country club, maids, and that pretty home of his. She is probably already planning on redecorating Cumberland as soon as I die. However, I have a very long life ahead me. That girl will need to check her attitude or I will not leave Oliver this house."

Kelly Copeland was not soft. Deborah had to admit it didn't look as if she had much affection for her husband, or even her sweet and bubbly daughter, Sarah. She seemed indifferent and on occasion she could be shockingly cold. Oliver doted on her and she reacted as if she were a queen and he a mere jester. The small woman was pretty, though, at least on the outside, and always impeccably coiffed. Deborah wrote the monthly checks for her hairdresser, manicurist, masseuse, personal trainer, shopper, and maid. Deborah would not expect anything less than perfection from the woman.

Simon Copeland was the second son, the brat prince of the family. He had not been raised to take part in the Copeland Enterprises. It seemed he had been raised to be unemployed, royalty without responsibility. He spent his time spending his trust fund, attending parties, and posing for social media, magazines, and the newspaper's social pages. He showed up to the house most Sunday mornings for family brunch, and had lunch with his mother and brother nearly every Wednesday. Mrs. Copeland didn't discuss his activities, the endless string of anorexic models he called girlfriends, or the rumors of alcohol and drug binges. She spoke about him as if he were the dearest, most munificent, and most noble of men. It was no secret that she favored her younger son.

At two-thirty, Deborah stepped into Mrs. Copeland's sitting room. "Excuse me, Mrs. Copeland. I have a meeting with Mr. Boothby at three, then I will stop at Oliver's house and give Franklin the payroll. Is there anything else you need today?"

The woman looked up, letting her lips curl ever so slightly in the approximation of a smile. "No, dear." Yet she continued to give her instructions. "I want linen invitations, remember. Please hand out the checks yourself. I don't want Franklin doing that anymore, except for the out-staff. Stop by the bank and order Oliver some more checks as well. He wants the gold embossed business premier checks, not the business standard. And please let Charlotte know that the Sumners are coming for dinner tomorrow. Oh, and tell Franklin to remind Oliver and Kelly to be here tomorrow, dressed for dinner, at seven. I will see you in the morning, Miss Wade."

HOME

Deborah stepped into her little house, which was really just a mother-in-law cottage behind the fancy home of her landlord, Jacob Armel. Her place was really no more than a studio apartment with a loft. The bottom floor was made up of a small kitchen, breakfast table, bookshelf, closet, love seat, chair and ottoman, with a door to the bathroom and shower. The loft had a bed, dresser, and closet. She used the laundry room behind the main house and had full use of the swimming pool. It was a nice little cottage, a haven that was her very own space.

   She took off her heels and sighed in relief at being barefoot. She then carefully removed her skirt and blouse and hung them up in the "to be cleaned" section of her closet. When she had begun working for Mrs. Copeland she had five business outfits, one afternoon dress, and one evening dress. Yet when her employer had seen her repeat the first outfit on her second Monday, she immediately took Deborah shopping. The new clothes filled both the upstairs and downstairs closets, and gave her enough variety that Mrs. Copeland no longer had to be concerned with out-of-date, frequently worn, or inadequate clothing for her secretary. She insisted on dry cleaning as part of Deborah's salary, not as a kindness but as good management of her investment, and included a certificate once each month for another outfit from the boutique she frequented.

Deborah, of course, didn't mind, but she preferred her jeans and comfortable shoes to the heels and skirts her job required. Now she changed into sweatpants, t-shirt, and socks. She put a can of soup on the stove, pulled out her tattered copy of *Jane Eyre*, curled up in her chair, and reread the story of the plain but dream-filled governess.

It wasn't even an hour later when a knock came at the door. She opened it to find Jacob standing there dressed in only a swimsuit, even in the cool of the April evening. Jacob Armel was a very handsome man of about thirty years, with thick blonde hair, bright green eyes, and an expensive year-round tan. He clearly knew he was a good-looking man. He took pains with his appearance yet did not convey conceit. He had the sort of wealth the Lady of Cumberland Manor would approve of: old money, and plenty of it. Deborah didn't know many details about what he did for a living, only that he was some sort of executive with a Manhattan-based firm that his great grandfather had begun.

"Mr, Armel," she said, surprised at seeing the nearly naked man at her door. "What can I do for you?"

"Deborah, I'm about to go for a swim, and

I thought maybe you would join me?"

She didn't know what to say. She liked him, but a swim made her uncomfortable. Really, the idea of having to talk to him and spend time alone with him made her feel awkward. "Oh, thank you Mr. Armel," she said as she tried to think of an excuse. "But I am so busy! I have so much to get done. I took my work home with me tonight."

He looked a bit crestfallen for just a moment, then recovered. "Oh, well then, perhaps next time."

Deborah returned to her book, wondering if she had let herself down by not joining him for a swim and also feeling guilty over her lie. She had terrible anxiety when it came to spending time socializing with people, especially men. She wanted to go put on her swimsuit and enjoy the evening with Jacob, but couldn't make herself do it.

Deborah had always been very shy. For years she wondered what secrets she was missing that everyone else seemed to understand. She didn't know how to socialize, even how to have simple conversations. Until high school her social life had been nearly non-existent. She had gone through many days without uttering a single word except to tell the lunch lady whether she wanted the hot or cold lunch choice. Before high school, she had a single friend, Jackie, who lived down the street from her house. They didn't even attend the same school. Jackie's parents sent her to Good Shepherd Academy, so they were only able to see one another after school and on weekends.

Once Deborah started ninth grade, she decided to learn the secrets of conversation, so she could understand the cues she was not seeing and make some more friends. The best way she could think of was to take drama class and join the drama club. Deborah loved to read and had always acted out the books in her head anyway, so acting on a stage seemed a natural extension of that. It would open doors, or even just windows, for the person she was inside to show up on the outside.

More or less, it had worked. She was now very good at conversation, knew all the rules of courtesy, and was able to express herself more clearly, but she was still anxious about almost every encounter, particularly when it involved men and above all men she liked. As much as she would have liked to be brave, put on her swimsuit, and charm the striking Jacob Armel, she couldn't do it.

GOOD ROCKIN' TONIGHT

The next evening was Friday and Deborah had plans: her favorite rock band, Epsilon, was playing at the Inverness Club. Her VIP ticket included a meet and greet with the band, special seating, and an area by the stage for watching the show. Deborah laughed to herself as she looked in the mirror and decided Mrs. Copeland would definitely not approve of the skinny jeans, silver-linked chain belt, and thin blouse with a cami top showing through. Deborah's long dark hair hung loose and flowing rather than being bound into a tight professional style. Instead of designer heels she wore black heeled boots.

She arrived at the club, feeling quite stunning and self-assured right up until she was about to enter the venue. Butterflies filled her stomach, but she took a deep breath, put her confident face back on, and walked in. The VIP crowd was relatively small, just twenty people. They gathered in booths and seats marked off for their group. Soon Epsilon came into the room and the band members sat at a table. The question and answer period was Deborah's favorite. Although there were always the people who asked common questions, there were also people who asked great and interesting questions which Deborah would never have thought of. Deborah didn't ask any; she just listened. After the Q&A, the band spent time having conversations with the fans, signing autographs, and posing for pictures.

Deborah was minding her own business at a table, people-watching, as she generally did. She noticed Ash, the band's bass player and main songwriter, get up from a table and head somewhere. He looked over at Deborah, and paused, as if wondering why an attractive woman were sitting by herself rather than flocking around the band. Deborah tried to pretend she didn't notice him looking at her. Finally he seemed to make up his mind, and started walking toward Deborah.

Deborah watched the tall man walk over, and took a deep breath, trying to calm her pounding heart. His thick, dark, curly hair stopped just above his shoulders. His eyes were so dark they looked black, and they twinkled with a smile.

"Weren't you at the show last October at the Dew Drop Inn?" He didn't wait for a reply. "Can I bring you a piece of pizza or get you a drink?"

Deborah was so dazed she almost didn't answer. He remembered her from a concert six months before? He had noticed her? He was talking to her? Oh, yes, he needed an answer. "Yes; that was a great show. Um, no thanks, I'm not hungry."

"May I sit down?"

"Oh...sure... I mean, yes, please do."

Asher Levine sat down, ordered a drink, reminded Deborah that he drank for free, and ordered one for her as well. She accepted a white wine. The two talked for so long that Deborah began to worry she was keeping him from the other fans, but he assured her that was not the case. A few fans made their way to him and he signed autographs, posed for pictures, and chatted with people all the while staying next to Deborah, listening to her talk and making her feel as if he thought he were the lucky one.

At some point, the other band members came over and each ordered drinks and food. The fans, for the most part, let the band get their food in peace. Ash introduced Deborah to the rest of the band as if she were an old friend, "This is Christian, Frank, Brian, and Dave. Guys, this is Deborah." The band members were all were very kind. Long-haired Christian grabbed a poster from a nearby table, had all the guys sign it, and gave it to Deborah. Dave, the drummer, was diminutive but not shy, and ordered a second drink for Deborah as well as a tray of appetizers that he insisted she share. Suddenly, it was time for the band to retreat backstage and let the general audience into the club. Deborah was left with a tray full of wings, cheese sticks, and various unidentified fried foods.

The show was one of Deborah's all-time favorites. Epsilon played hard and passionately, and the crowd went wild. When

Dave broke a drumstick, he tossed it to Deborah, and when Brian dropped his pick, it too got tossed to her.

Although Deborah normally stayed well after concerts ended, she left quickly when this one finished, anxious about another encounter with Ash. Ash was one of the nicest men she had ever met, and she had even imagined he was flirting with her. She realized how silly she was to think that Ash had done anything more than show a little kindness to a fan. He was just a nice person, and Deborah knew she always let her avid reader's imagination run away from her. She didn't want him to think she had mistaken a charismatic rock star for anything other than that, and she definitely didn't want him to think she was a groupie. Although she wanted to talk to him again, her chest tightened in anxiety at the thought, and she didn't understand how it was possible to feel both of those things at the same time.

Deborah loved the feeling of the night, and driving back home from the club let her travel through an area unlike anything the town where she lived and worked. Belle Cay reminded Deborah of a movie set, where everything was pristine and orderly, made just for the wealthy. There were no fast food places, dive bars, or supermarkets. Instead it had cafes, cocktail bars, and gourmet markets. She laughed, remembering how surprised she had been to be shopping for groceries at the Greenwell's Market and hear Wagner and Mozart over the speakers instead of the muzak of Abba and Barry Manilow she was used to hearing.

She put her Epsilon CD in the car stereo and turned it up. Although she had just left the concert, finding out what a very nice guy Ash and the rest of the guys were made her enjoy the music even more. Now she listened to the songs he had written with a new appreciation that there was a real person behind the poetry.

It was about one-thirty in the morning when she got home, but Jacob was at the pool entertaining a beautiful dark-haired woman. Deborah managed to sneak past them since they were completely engrossed in one another. She stepped inside and unrolled the poster the band had signed for her. She wasn't an autograph collector, but it did feel special to have been given the gift without asking for it. With a smile, she rolled it up and put it in her hope chest with her most treasured possessions.

DIRTY LITTLE SECRET

Deborah was just about to enter the library when she heard Kelly yelling behind its thick door. "You are an imbecile! How can any person expect me to be with you? I'm the only one who will ever put up with you, and I have to say, I'm over it. What did I do to deserve being stuck with you?" There was a sound that might have been a slap. Deborah halted outside the door and took a step back, unsure what to do. Kelly continued her tirade. "I don't care what you want. People expect my husband to accompany me to the opera and I will not give them a reason to talk. If I am stuck in this sham of a marriage, you will keep up appearances and be my husband, at least in public!"

    Deborah needed to go into the library, but she had no desire to shame the couple for arguing. She looked around and saw Maria, one of the maids, headed toward some important job somewhere else in the house. "Excuse me, Maria." She called out a little too loudly. "Could you please ask Ian to bring me some tea in the library? Thank you." Maria gave her a strange look and assured her she would do so. Deborah opened the heavy door slowly and entered the library where Kelly and Oliver sat on separate ends of a couch. The normally cool Kelly sat straight-backed, cheeks red, with a newspaper open on her lap. Oliver looked a bit defeated, his eyes on the wall away from his seething wife, trying to catch his breath. Was there a red mark on his cheek?

Kelly put the paper aside. In a voice as icy as her gaze, she said, "I am going shopping, and I will eat lunch out today. Perhaps," she emphasized the word, "I'll meet you at home later." She stood up and walked out of the room without waiting for a response from Oliver.

Even as she was leaving, Oliver said, "Yes, darling. Enjoy your day. I'll see you this evening." Kelly was already gone.

Deborah had no idea what she should do. She wanted to give Oliver some privacy, but Mrs. Copeland had decided the family records had to be bound in leather. Deborah had been tasked with gathering, organizing, and packing everything for the printer; she had no choice but to be in the room. "How are you, Oliver?"

"Fine," he said quietly. He didn't move from the couch. His eyes remained on the wall, but he was clearly dejected, and it seemed to Deborah he was trying to gather his composure to mask his feelings. At last, with a steadier voice, he said, "And you, Miss Wade, how are you?"

"I'm well, thank you. Your mother wants me to organize the announcements from the family births and marriages and such. Do you know where those are? Perhaps it would be entertaining if you helped me put them in order." Although she doubted it would be much fun, it might take his mind off the mysterious argument, or it might give him the chance to talk about it.

He looked a little panicked. "No, I, um... I can't... I mean... I am just not in the mood to look at memories right now. But I will stay and keep you company."

Ian entered carrying a tea service, set it down on the table, and offered to pour. Oliver stood and said, "Thank you, Ian; I'll pour. Miss Wade?"

"Thank you," she said, taking her cup and adding her own milk and plenty of sugar. She took the cup to the desk, found the boxes of announcements, and began the tedious work of putting them in order by subject and date. The work would have been more interesting with help, but Oliver wasn't paid to do this and she was.

"How are you enjoying your work here? Mother is so pleased to have you." He picked up the newspaper Kelly had put down, folded it, and placed it on the table.

"I like it here. I never get bored. I certainly enjoy Cumberland and, of course, all the family. You must have loved growing up in such a lovely place. I bet you could tell some stories."

"Yes," said Oliver, without adding a story. "Where is your family? Do you live near them?"

Deborah sighed. She wasn't sure she wanted to talk about her family, and she tried to think of an answer that would not reveal the pain associated with their estrangement. "I grew up in Florida. I left for college when I was eighteen and never looked back. I just loved Connecticut. I had to stay."

Oliver looked at Deborah. "I'm really quite sorry you had to hear Kelly earlier. She wants me to go to the opera. I don't enjoy it." He paused and offered an excuse for his wife. "She's been under some stress."

"I'm sorry to have interrupted I wish I could have left you so you could have worked it out."

"I was never going to get out of going. I shouldn't have even mentioned it. She's had it hard lately. I only want to make her happy."

Deborah wondered if Kelly had ever been happy, or even could be. By chance, the next item in the first record box was a newspaper article announcing Oliver and Kelly's engagement. Oliver was young, robust and happy in the photo. Kelly stood next to him, looking more triumphant than happy. Although Oliver was still handsome, he was more slender than he had been then. He looked frail and pale now rather than ruddy and healthy. Deborah knew his accident had been serious, changing the athlete into a patient, but she didn't know the details, and although she was curious, she didn't feel she had a right to ask. The announcement was placed in the file next to the wedding invitation. Soon she came upon Sarah's birth announcement and set that in its proper place. Oliver remained quiet for some time as Deborah made progress on the job. The records were not quite as disorganized as she imagined they might be.

Oliver sat, pensively drinking his tea. He poured more for each of them. Deborah watched him limp across the room, carefully carrying the delicate tea pot. She appreciated his gracious manners. How did this man ever end up with someone like Kelly?

Suddenly the tranquility was spoiled as Simon burst into the room. "Hello! Ollie, I've been looking all over for you. Debbie, how are you?" He didn't wait for a response. "So, Ollie, I need a favor. I'm meeting Cyan tomorrow at La Corbeille à Pain and I need you to cover for me with Mom. I was supposed have lunch with her. If you meet Mom, she'll forgive me for standing her up." He poured himself a gin and downed it in one swallow, then poured a second.

"Sure. Where?" Oliver said unenthusiastically. Deborah knew that Cyan, who was an exotic dancer, was not someone Mrs. Copeland endorsed, and it would be up to Oliver to explain his brother's whereabouts.

"Thanks! Park Café. Don't forget Park Café at one. Deb, you'll remind him please?" Simon finished his drink and left the room without giving her a chance to answer.

Deborah smiled at Oliver. "That's kind of you. I've heard your mother talk about Cyan. She is not a fan. But Simon doesn't really date the kind of women your mother likes."

"He doesn't date in hopes of getting married; he goes out with the intention of staying single. Listen, would you join us for lunch? I would appreciate it. You have to eat anyway, right? Your presence will soften the reaction. Kelly will still be mad at me."

"Sure, I'll be there. I'll make the reservations."

The next day Deborah walked through the garden, taking in the scents of the various flowers and watching bees move from one blossom to another. Though she was required to be at Cumberland every weekday, she was not required to actually work each hour she spent there. Often Mrs. Copeland would be out, or would simply have no need of her services, and Deborah was frequently needed to attend an event or do other work in the evenings or on weekends, so it was understood that her schedule was flexible. Mrs. Copeland wanted Deborah present just in case she was needed, but gave her free reign of the estate as long as she stayed ready and available. Today was such a day.

Her mind was stayed on Jacob Armel. She imagined him falling in love with her and sweeping her away to Paris, Rome, and London with him. She knew he would never consider her more than a tenant or an acquaintance. Even friendship seemed a hope well beyond the possibilities. She had rarely seen a man as good looking as he was. His smile seemed so genuine, and though she barely knew him, it made her think he was funny and kind. She imagined him as the nobleman who would see in her the nobility that matched his own, the personality that could equal his. She envisioned that he would know it was her and only her who could ever make him happy. He could be the Fitzwilliam Darcy to her Elizabeth.

Her reverie was broken by the sound of Oliver's voice on the phone. "...two dozen roses to my home address...yes...it should read, 'Looking forward to the opera.' Thank you."

Deborah walked away in another direction. Oliver was always buying Kelly gifts as if he could buy her love instead of her affected affections. To Deborah it seemed clear Kelly didn't love Oliver. Maybe there was no such thing as true love. Life was not a romantic novel like *Pride and Prejudice*. It was real, and people married, divorced, or refused to divorce for things like money, homes, and need. People pretended to be in love so they could pretend they were better than other people.

Her phone chimed to remind her that the car was leaving for the restaurant in fifteen minutes. She called Oliver to remind him. Oliver never texted; he was sort of old-fashioned that way. Communication was either in person or over the phone. That was something else she liked about him. He was a gentleman who did not give in to social pressures. As apathetic as Kelly was toward Oliver, he lavished gifts on her. She wouldn't accept his love, but she was happy to accept gifts.

The restaurant was a quiet little café inside the Belle Cay hotel just behind the row of exclusive boutiques on the Cay's main thoroughfare. Deborah felt like an intruder in the cafe; she supposed her presence was intended to moderate the harsh reactions expected from the two Mrs. Copelands. Kelly was her usual cold self, and showed none of the fiery anger she had thrown at her husband the day before. Mrs. Copeland was angry at Simon's choice of a stripper over her, yet she refrained from chastising her wayward son, instead directing her anger at the woman she called a money-grubbing tart, and at Oliver, whom she blamed for letting Simon go with Cyan. "It will be your fault, Oliver, when he marries someone with such a questionable character. She or someone with a similarly silly name will walk him down the aisle just to get his money."

Oliver glanced ever so slightly at Kelly before he looked at his mother, "Yes; we wouldn't want something like that to happen to him."

Catherine Copeland ignored the statement. "She will ruin his reputation. He won't be able to run the foundation, and all that money for charity will be lost. We help women like Cyan come out of prostitution; we don't reward them for their efforts." She took a bite of her steak tartare and continued. "You need not be helping him find these frivolous loose women, or covering for him. You are the older brother. Live up to that, Oliver. You may not be as strong as you once were, but you do not have to be feeble. If you cannot be the man you are meant to be, at least have the decency to pretend to be that man."

Kelly gave a quick hard laugh. "Feeble, ha!" then in a voice meant to sound as if it were under her breath she said, "Feeble-minded and pathetic."

Mrs. Copeland turned her sharp glare toward her daughter in law. "Behave," she whispered.

Oliver moved the food around on his plate and set his fork down. Then he folded his napkin and placed it on the plate. "Mother, you're right. I let Simon get away with too much. I spoiled him. I should have set boundaries and instead I gave him everything he ever wanted."

Deborah swallowed her food and watched nervously to see how Mrs. Copeland would react to the veiled insult.

"Dear," she said, "You may not choose to remember it, but Yale was not an inexpensive or second-rate gift. Your education, the car you drove, the house you lived in, even the house you live in now, the vacations, and all the rest were all things you wanted. I made sure you had them. Should I have withheld any of it?"

Kelly spoke up, changing the subject. "*Les Troyens* is the first opera of the season. We're looking forward to seeing it. The papers are raving about the new ingénue. Her voice is supposed to rival Katherine Jenkins."

Suddenly the three of them acted as if the previous conversation had not taken place. Kelly and Oliver pretended they both loved opera and were a happy couple. Mrs. Copeland feigned interest in their upcoming social calendar. Deborah felt she must have missed some crucial lesson in conversation, and wondered if she would ever understand these people.

BOYS KEEP SWINGING

June brought the Arthur Copeland Foundation Art Auction to Belle Cay. The wealthiest people from New England attended the black tie affair, which included cocktails, dinner, and the lively auction itself. People donated works, artists created pieces, and a great deal of money was raised for the various charities under the foundation. Deborah had never seen anything like the pretentious exhibitions of the guests. She doubted any of them knew or cared about the charities they were supporting. They just wanted to look good and show off their money for one another. She saw Jacob Armel with a voluptuous blonde in a dress that might as well have had solid gold dollar signs embroidered on it. It likely cost more than the painting Jacob had won, and more than a month's salary of the wait staff of the event.

Simon, his anonymous date, Oliver, Kelly, and Catherine Copeland were seated at a table near the center of the room, along with a few other socialites. Deborah joined them and was introduced to Mrs. Clark Templeton and her son Declan. Deborah wondered if wealthy women missed their first names or the identities they had before their wedding days. Mrs. Templeton was in her sixties or seventies, with thick white hair and the pretty face of a woman who could afford a facial every month. Her son was possibly in his thirties, but it was difficult to tell because he had Down syndrome. He smiled at Deborah but did not speak when introduced. Instead he turned to Simon. "Have you ever dated the same woman twice?"

Rather than return his rudeness directly, Simon used socially acceptable passive-aggressiveness. "I do, but unlike some men, I have a long list of beauties with whom to enjoy my time. Where's your date, Declan?"

No one at the table acknowledged the masked clash had taken place. Declan and his mother offered courtesies and moved on to another table. Once they were gone, Kelly immediately talked about the pity of having a son like that. Her words were unsympathetic and cruel. Mrs. Copeland agreed it was a pity to have a child who could never grow up. Kelly took the elder's agreement and ran with it, discussing the misfortune of handicaps. Simon laughed. Oliver stood up abruptly and said, "I'm going to get a drink." He left the table as swiftly as his limp allowed. Kelly rolled her eyes and enjoyed a bonding moment with her mother-in-law.

Deborah wished she had not come. Her presence had not been required, but she had thought it rude to turn down the invitation, and she was also curious about the event. Now, though, she was sure she had made the wrong choice. Mrs. Copeland turned away from Kelly to her assistant. "Jacob Armel is a very handsome man. But, Deborah, he is not right for you. Don't even dream of dating him."

Deborah was stunned, not only by the hurtful words but also by the fact that her feelings had been so apparent. Did her boss really consider her too low to date a wealthy man? Did Deborah wear her thoughts on her face so clearly? "Thank you. I am going to get some fresh air." She stepped outside into the warm night and wondered if Jacob had seen her leave. If he had, he didn't follow. She didn't know if she should stay or not. She was tired, unimpressed by the manners of polite society, and a little bored. She had hoped the extravagance would keep her interested but soon enough a $5,000 dress looked the same as a $10,000 dress. After a few minutes, Oliver came to stand by her side. She tried to cover up a yawn.

"I feel the same way," Oliver told her. "I know it's pompous of me to be bored, but I am. How long can I be expected to feign interest in where Buffy is summering this year and why Chip has decided not to play polo?" He spoke the latter part of his question with a put-on nasal voice.

Deborah laughed. "I have no reason be a snob, but I think maybe I am above these people. You are too, Oliver."

"They're not all like that. Some are really kind and almost down to earth. It's the few who spoil the bunch. I can never remember who is whom. Buffy could be Tiffy and Biff could be Chip. I only know that if I decide my mother is the most aristocratic of them, I've got it right. I think she might pretend to be more of a snob than she really is when she's with these people."

Deborah loved that he wouldn't speak against his mother. "Would it be rude if I went home? Would anyone notice?"

His kind eyes looked directly into hers. "I would notice, but I won't tell. Go home. I'll go get your purse and wrap." He went back inside and she went to the valet to get her car.

Driving away from the auction, Deborah was not quite as tired as she had felt before. It was just after 9:00. She felt pretty in her evening dress, so she drove to the Belle Cay Community Park and decided to take a walk. The air was warm and smelled of the many flowers growing throughout the park. Apart from Deborah, the park was deserted. Normally she would have expected to see a couple or two on the commons, strolling the paths, or talking by the fountain. Tonight it appeared people were otherwise engaged.

Faint music floated toward her. Deborah looked for its source and found it came from La Taverna Giardino, an upscale tavern across the street from the park. Of course, everything in Belle Cay was upscale. To live here, one would think there was no such thing as middle class; people were either rich or servants of the rich. In reality that was not the case, as there were business owners and employees, but they existed to serve the wealthy the same as the maids, chefs, and butlers. She entered the bar and saw a duo performing pop songs on the stage. A young man with long brown hair played an acoustic guitar, and at his feet was a small black box Deborah recognized as an electronic percussion instrument. A girl with short red hair and a bohemian dress played a keyboard.

Deborah sat down at a table off to the side, ordered a club soda, and enjoyed the music. A man with dark blonde hair and an orange tan suddenly appeared at the table and sat down. "May I buy you a drink, darling?" His voice had the flat and nasal tone she might hear from Thurston Howell III. It was nearly the same voice Oliver had just used to mock the people at the art auction.

She hated it when people called her darling, sweetie, or other so-called endearments when they didn't know her. She didn't want to be rude, but she didn't want to talk to him either. "No, thank you. I have a drink coming."

He sat down anyway, undeterred. "My name is Chip Masterson."

She nearly burst out laughing as she wondered if he would be playing polo this summer. Chip took the stifled laugh as a smile of encouragement, and when the waitress brought Deborah's club soda, he ordered her a second one to ensure it was he who would be buying. According to the steps in the social dance Deborah had learned, that meant Deborah was obliged to chat with him, but she had no idea what to talk about. "Nice to meet you. I'm Deborah." She would at least give him a chance.

"Darling, you look beautiful! Perhaps the most beautiful woman in this bar or any other. What brings you here looking so angelic?"

His over-the-top flattery did not charm her; rather, his continued use of the unwanted endearment irritated her. Yet she couldn't be rude. "I was taking a walk and heard the music."

Chip kept talking, filling up the silences with meaningless chatter. Each time Deborah thought she might enjoy the company, he called her darling or dear and ruined the moment. As soon as she finished the second club soda, he tried to order her another. She knew he thought she was drinking something with alcohol; perhaps he wanted to get her drunk. He lifted his finger to order but she stood up, feigned fatigue, and left the tavern.

ROAM

It was a bright Saturday morning, and it was Deborah's favorite kind of Saturday: the kind where there was nothing on her calendar. She went about her morning routine humming with joy and wondering how best to spend her free day. Belleshore was a lovely town near Belle Cay which hosted a large farmer's market every Saturday and Sunday. The beautiful weather was making the farmer's market sound like the beginning of a great day.

She arrived in Belleshore and intentionally parked several blocks away from the marketplace to enjoy a stroll through the town center. There were tables piled with fresh fruits and vegetables of every variety. Vendors sold wares from handmade jewelry to honey. Deborah bought a fresh cold-pressed vegetable juice and meandered from booth to booth. She was looking through the paintings of a local artist, admiring the intricate and almost childlike quality of the paintings, when Jacob stepped up next to her. He carried a bag with a doll sticking out of the top.

"Hello, Deborah!" he said with a big smile. "I'm so glad to have run into a friend. How are you?"

"I'm well, thank you, Mr. Armel."

"Jacob, please," he interrupted.

"Jacob," she repeated, with a smile that not only lifted her cheeks but reddened them as well. "I'm just enjoying the market and the fresh air. What are you doing here?"

"I'm in the mood for a salad and thought I would buy some vegetables for it." He noticed Deborah's glance at his bag. "And buying a gift for my niece." He waited a moment and added, "Deborah, do you like salad?"

Now she knew her cheeks were red. "Yes. Yes, I do."

"Good. Then you'll join me this evening on the pool deck for Salad a la Armel?"

"What, may I ask, is Salad a la Armel?"

"I will find out after I buy the ingredients, and you will find out when you join me for dinner."

She laughed. "Yes. That sounds adventurous." She had no idea what to say next and suddenly became engrossed in looking at a painting of a brightly colored city with flying saucers dotting the sky. Mrs. Copeland was wrong; Deborah could date someone like Jacob.

"Well, I had better go find those ingredients. I'll see you this evening at 7:00." He left and disappeared into the crowd.

Deborah floated through the rows of vendors, but now, instead of seeing the lemonade stand or the woman churning butter, she was trying to decide what she would wear. This called for a new outfit, something special that didn't look forced, something nice but not too fancy. She headed to Belleshore Mall where the prices were more her level than the Belle Cay boutiques.

That evening Deborah looked at herself in

her new cream linen pants and matching jacket with a blue linen tank top under the jacket. She tried to decide between the cream heels or the sandals, and decided the heels looked nicer. It was 6:53. She checked her make-up, sat down and rechecked the time. It was 6:54. With a deep breath she willed herself to be calm. At last she stood up, looked at her make-up again, reapplied some gloss, and walked outside, down the little sidewalk over to the pool deck. Jacob was nowhere to be seen, but there was a table set for two and a rose on a plate by one of the seats.

She smiled, picking up and smelling the pink rose. As she was taking in the perfume, Jacob emerged from the house carrying a bottle of wine. He caught her eye and gave her that great smile of his. His tanned skin, blonde hair and green eyes were enhanced by the white woven pants and soft gold cabana shirt he wore. "Jacob, you look beautiful!" Her cheeks turned red again as the words left her mouth.

He laughed and his eyes twinkled. "I think I was about to tell you the very same thing. Thank you. I wasn't going for beautiful. Maybe very handsome, but not beautiful. Standing next to you, though, I cannot compare. You are overwhelmingly gorgeous, stunning."

"Thank you," she said. She looked into the rose and smelled it once more, aware of his eyes on her.

"Please have a seat. Would you like some wine?" He poured the wine, and they both sat down and drank. Deborah was certain she had never tasted wine this good before. She wanted to ask what it was, but felt she was probably supposed to know if it were chardonnay or cabernet, and didn't want to give away her lack of culture.

Soon a young man came with a large bowl of salad. He offered Deborah the bowl, and she served herself some escarole with an assortment of vegetables chopped perfectly into it. Jacob served himself some, and then the two ate. "I couldn't decide which vegetables to put in, so I put them all!" Jacob told her with a winsome smile. "So I supposed Salad a la Armel is salad with everything. It might be too much, but then again, I might be too much,"

"It is really good!"

"I made it myself, including the dressing. When I was a child I would spend afternoons with Ms. Truman, the cook. She was really a wonderful chef. She taught me very well, let me help, and made sure that I knew the difference between julienne, chiffonade, and paysanne."

"I don't know the difference." Even as the words left her mouth she realized she shouldn't have said them. Jacob would know she wasn't as cultured as him. She had let her guard down, allowed herself to get caught up in the moment, and spoken without thinking.

"I'll be happy to teach you." He touched her hand.

She blushed again and hoped the light wasn't showing her red face. After the salad was eaten and the bottle of wine emptied,

Jacob led Deborah into his living room. She could only describe it as grand. It was decorated in shades of cream and gold, with a grand piano, large couches and settees, sculptures, and a marble fire place. He took her from sculpture to sculpture explaining who the artist was, what the sculpture portrayed, and asking her opinion. Deborah really didn't know enough about art to be comfortable offering opinions much deeper than, "It's lovely!" or "I like this one."

He was not put off by her artistic inexperience, and seemed to enjoy describing the finer points of art to his eager student for as long as she wanted to listen. Deborah was stunned when she looked down at Jacob's watch and saw that it was midnight. "Thank you so much for a brilliant evening," she said. "I think it might be past my bedtime."

Jacob walked her to her door, pecked her on the cheek and left her.

Rather than going to bed, the happy young woman danced through her home singing "I Feel Pretty," as if she were the star of *West Side Story*. Even though it had become apparent she was not on the same rung of the social ladder as Jacob, he had enjoyed her company. Images of dating this seemingly perfect man filled Deborah's head, and she imagined what it would be like introducing her boyfriend to people. Her bliss would not let her hear the nagging voices of her past which tried to tell her that Jacob was too good to be true. Nothing, in her eyes, could mar his perfect veneer.

NEW YORK

Epsilon was advertising a concert at a club in New York, and Deborah decided she was going to take the trip and make a weekend of it. "Mrs. Copeland, I have plans on the weekend of the 16th. If possible I would like that Friday off, so I can make a trip to New York City."

"Are you going to the city alone? I don't like the idea of that."

"Yes, I am planning on going by myself, but I'll be fine." She was unsure if Mrs. Copeland was more concerned for her protection or her propriety.

"I wanted to take a shopping trip anyway. Why don't I make it that weekend? You can go with me. We can go on the Thursday." She didn't wait for Deborah's acquiescence; she assumed it. "Make reservations for two suites at The St. Regis for four nights. Arrange the jet as well. You'll work for me on Thursday and Monday. The other days will be yours, but I do hope you might let me show you some of the sights."

Deborah was amazed. She was going to

stay at the St. Regis, fly on a private jet, and see the New York they showed in movies. "Mrs. Copeland, that is more than kind! Thank you."

"Oh no, dear, it is selfish. I need to go shopping, and taking advantage of a trip you were going to take anyway gives me a reason to go. I think we need to get you another evening dress before we leave."

Deborah knew better than to debate Mrs. Copeland's claim that she needed a new dress. She planned on dining at the finest restaurants, and that meant she should be dressed for the part. The outfits were just another job requirement, like a costume. That she got to feel like a princess when she wore them was especially nice. Mrs. Copeland gave her the list of places she would be dining so that Deborah could make the reservations, and she invited Deborah to join her for any that she chose to.

As soon as Mrs. Copeland had finished speaking, Deborah went to her office to make all the arrangements. Her head was already filled with visions of Broadway and Times Square, of places so dazzling that even the jaded rich raised their eyebrows in appreciation. The wait until that Thursday would be excruciating.

THE SOUND OF MUSIC

That evening Cumberland was hosting a dinner party in honor of Mr. and Mrs. Sumner's cousin, Thomas Sumner, a classical pianist who was going to play a selection for the guests after the meal. He was a celebrated up-and-comer in the music world. Deborah knew the guests included a record company executive and a communications company executive. It would be quite the evening.

Charlotte, the head housekeeper, was out of town, and Ian was busy with ensuring the dinner party details, so Deborah had stepped in to make sure the maids were preparing the music room and parlor for the evening's events. The music room was being arranged to accommodate the mini-concert. Four maids cleaned the already clean rooms, another two tidied up the dining room, and Ian oversaw the table settings. Deborah was not taking part in the stuffy dinner, since it had nothing to do with her job. The formality and intimacy made her feel as if she were under a microscope. A cheeseburger was more her style than five courses of forced and pretentious conversation. She would attend the concert afterward, and looked forward to hearing Mr. Sumner play.

As time for the dinner approached, Deborah retreated to a guest room to get dressed. When she returned downstairs to see if Ian needed any help, she came across an unhappy Kelly walking out of the sitting room and into the parlor. The woman stormed past her, glanced at her, and did not acknowledge her. Deborah walked into the sitting room and saw Oliver pacing from door to window and back again. "Is everything okay?" she asked hesitantly. She wasn't sure she felt like dealing with the drama, but she did care about Oliver. He sometimes seemed so delicate, so easily breakable. If she could somehow give him her strength, she would. He realized that she and Oliver had become good friends since she had begun working at Cumberland.

He looked up, startled but relieved to see Deborah. "Yes, it's fine." He laughed, although it sounded false and the smile didn't reach his eyes. "I wore the Armani, when she wanted me to wear the Givenchy. I must have forgotten." He shook his head, gave another fake smile and subconsciously touched his cheek which appeared red to Deborah.

She wondered if Kelly had slapped him again, and then wondered if she slapped him often. Could Kelly really be violent? She always appeared so cool, except for the time Deborah had overheard their argument. Was she supposed to ask? Was it right? She hated to think that Oliver was being hurt. "Oliver, did Kelly hit you?"

"No! No! She gets very frustrated with me. I'm not fashionable. I don't even know which of my tuxedos are Givenchy or Armani or Ralph Lauren. It's important to her. I let her down. She wants to impress people."

Deborah had to believe him, but she wasn't sure if she did. "Violence, whether it comes from a man or a woman, is wrong."

"I know that." He gave that short fake laugh again. "That tiny woman could never hurt me. She has a loud bark, that's all." He absentmindedly stroked his cheek when he spoke.

Thomas Sumner played the piano beautifully, and Deborah was enraptured. She sat in the back of the room listening to the complicated composition pour out of his fingertips. The small crowd sat equally captivated. Catherine Copeland smiled with as much pride as the Sumners.

Kelly did not appear to be upset with her husband at all. She sat close to him with her arm wrapped around his. Perhaps it was the music that had soothed the beast. Deborah thought it was more likely that she was putting on a show for the people in the room. She guessed they bought it too.

THE GOOD LIFE

The two women stepped off the jet into a waiting Bentley. Deborah had spent the time on the jet comfortably double-checking the foundation accounts. Mrs. Copeland trusted her accountant, but kept measures in place to assure honesty. Now Deborah could relax in the car and look at New York with a tourist's eyes. She took in the height of the buildings, the chaotic sounds which somehow became the symphony of the city, and the constant rush of people everywhere. Before she knew it they arrived at the hotel. She had only ever seen pictures of the St. Regis before. It was an aristocratic heaven out of an Edwardian dream in the midst of the bustling city. The door was opened by a smiling doorman. The luggage was brought in by a pleasant bell boy who led the women to their suites.

Deborah was too excited to be tired. She entered the room and pretended that the lavish furnishings were common to her. The picture of decorum, she quietly thanked the bell boy, handed him a tip she hoped was appropriately generous, and watched him leave. When she was sure he was no longer within hearing distance, she squealed in delight and fell on the comfortable king bed. The room was more luxurious than she had ever imagined, and no corner of it escaped her marveling gaze. Deborah almost didn't know what to do first. Should she unpack, take a bath, or write a letter to Jackie, the only connection with her previous home that she chose to keep intact?

She decided to go to Mrs. Copeland's room next door and unpack her clothes for her. "What a lovely hotel!" Deborah exclaimed. "It is much nicer than any hotel I could have chosen. My room is very nice. Thank you, Mrs. Copeland."

"My pleasure, Deborah," said her boss. "Please confirm our dinner reservations. I will meet you at the car at seven-thirty. The rest of the day is yours."

Deborah returned to her room, unpacked, got her camera, and decided to explore some of the surrounding city like the undignified tourist she was before returning to take a very long bubble bath and get dressed for dinner that evening.

I WILL REMEMBER YOU

Mrs. Copeland had insisted Deborah take a limo to the concert, and Deborah was relieved that she wouldn't have to brave the subway alone. She went very early to the neighborhood bar, which was not located anywhere close to the hotel at all, first because she had a VIP/meet-and-greet ticket and second because she wanted to see this different and less ritzy section of New York. She had her camera with her and tried as much as possible to immerse herself in the grittier culture she knew to be more real than the opulence of the rest of her trip.

The limo dropped her off in front of the club, but Deborah didn't stay there. Instead she walked down the street and found a deli that looked good, picking up a pastrami sandwich and sitting at a table near the window of the tiny delicatessen. It seemed like the kind of place that represented the real New York, so Deborah dug in her bag for her camera. While she was looking down, she heard a familiar voice.

"Deborah? Is that really you? I am so happy to see you!"

She looked up to see Ash. "Hi! I'm in town for the show. I'm so happy to see you too." She was worried it may not have come through in her voice, but she really was thrilled to see him. Her heart leaped at the idea of spending some time with someone who just seemed to appreciate her.

"Let me get my food. May I join you?"

"By all means, please do," she said with exuberance. Now that she had her good camera out, she wanted to get a picture taken with Ash. At the same time, she didn't want to come on too strong. In the end she decided against it.

Ash returned to the table and asked if he could take a selfie with her for Instagram. She said yes, but for some reason it bothered her, as if she were being relegated to fan instead of friend. Brian came in at that moment and was included in the selfie before he too went to get his food.

"I'm so happy to see you, Deborah," Ash said. He seemed genuinely joyful at the idea of spending time with her, and his interest in her dispelled her doubts about being seen as a fan instead of a friend. He asked questions and filled Brian in on details she had shared the last time they had talked. By the time the sandwiches were gone, Deborah had told them all about moving to Connecticut, working for the Copelands, and coming to New York.

"We have about an hour until sound check," Ash told her. "What are you doing before the show?"

"I'm doing a little exploring, taking some

pictures, that kind of thing."

"Can I join you?"

"I would love that!" Deborah said happily.

Brian said, "I have a few things I want to do before tonight. I think Dave wanted to talk to me. May I bow out?" He looked at Deborah for the question, but then gave Ash a slight wink.

"I'm sorry you won't be joining us. Maybe we can talk more later," Deborah said.

On their walk, Deborah asked Ash about his life. Ash described his large family; he was the second eldest of seven children. She also learned he was the music minister at a church and a graphic designer. "There is no way I could make a living from the band. We have records and they sell well enough, but we're too alternative to be really famous. We don't even have a record deal." His watch beeped and he said, "It's time to get back for the sound check. Want to come?"

Of course she did. She sat at the bar and listened to the surprisingly tedious process of checking each instrument, microphone, speaker, and sound level. Then Epsilon disappeared to somewhere backstage, and Deborah was then left alone to watch other bands' sound checks as the staff went through pre-opening procedures for the bar.

Before long Brian, Ash, Christian, Dave, and Frank were back out in the bar. All but Ash went to a table near the back of the room and began setting up the merchandise. Ash joined Deborah and invited her to watch them set up the merch table before the meet-and-greet was scheduled to begin. She enjoyed watching the guys joke back and forth with one another.

Frank was the most reserved of the men in person, though funnily enough he was the most animated of them on stage. During the shows he whipped his very long hair around, danced, and acted like what Deborah pictured when she imagined a rocker. Dave, though the smallest of them, had a big personality. Maybe drummers knew that being in the back meant they had to shine through in other ways. Brian was the lead singer, and was just as charismatic as Deborah imagined him to be. Christian was the lead guitarist; he was funny and seemed to have a joke ready for every occasion. Asher played bass, was second singer, and wrote the majority of the band's songs. Brian and Ash were the band's unofficial co-leaders.

The show was as good as she hoped, and this time she waited around afterward. She joined Epsilon and another band called Priests After Melchizedek for a late night breakfast at a nearby diner. She no longer feared these people were not her friends. Epsilon and Priests After Melchizedek were doing a concert at another club in New York the next night, or rather later that day, since it was two thirty in the morning. Ash took the chance to invite Deborah to go sightseeing with him after they'd had the chance to get some rest. Ash's good friend Jim Ramirez, the lead singer of the Priests, also wanted to come, along with his wife Andrea, the band's drummer. It would be a small group, and it sounded to Deborah like a perfect way to spend the day until the band was due for their sound set up and sound check at five in the afternoon.

HOLIDAY

Mrs. Copeland was not upset at all about Deborah's choice to go sightseeing with her new friends. "I will not want for company. I have many friends in the city, and just as many invitations. I think I will spend the day with Elana Arcola. Will I see you at dinner?"

"I don't think so; I am probably going to go see the band again tonight. If I do change my plans, I'll let you know." The more time Deborah spent with her employer, the more she got to like the woman. Although Mrs. Copeland had a dignified exterior and often acted even more of a snob than she already was, Deborah had begun to see there was genuine care and concern somewhere inside the woman. Mrs. Copeland had always taken care of her sons, and her staff, including Deborah. Maybe she wasn't the nicest person in the world, but she could be kind if she really put her mind to it. At least that's what Deborah truly believed.

Deborah realized Mrs. Copeland had such a responsibility to live up to in society and was always expected to conform to a certain set of standards. Moreover, the woman had been privileged from birth. Her family could not remember a time when they were not wealthy. Deborah knew the woman had more money than the rest of her staff could spend in several lifetimes.

Deborah met Ash, Jim, and Andrea at a coffee shop, and the three left for their day of fun. They went to Times Square and posed with three Supermans, The Naked Cowboy, and a Marilyn Monroe impersonator. Deborah was amazed by the sheer volume of people in the place. The group traveled to the Empire State building next and went to the observation deck to take in the jaw-dropping vista.

Deborah forgot that she was expected to behave a certain way, and just had fun being herself. She didn't even remember to be nervous. The four of them laughed and talked as they walked along Fifth Avenue. They took a cab to Battery Park, admired the Statue of Liberty, and ate hot dogs from a food cart. They took hundreds of photos filled with genuine smiles and not a single stiff pose.

LOST BOY

Although Simon endeavored to remain unemployed, he was on the Arthur Copeland Foundation's board of directors and would one day be the board president. He was required to attend the board meetings, and did so grudgingly. Deborah attended them as well, to take personal notes for Mrs. Copeland. That day the meeting was being held at the Belle Cay Hotel. Simon rode to the meeting in the limo with his mother and Deborah.

He drank coffee which smelled suspiciously like Irish cream to Deborah. She knew from experience that he was not a morning person. The mornings were the only times he didn't seem to express every thought that entered his head. His eyes were toward the window, but he wasn't looking outward. His gaze was directed inward and whatever he saw, felt, or thought was being kept to himself, except for the faintly sad look on his face. He took a drink of his coffee and turned his attention to his mother as she spoke.

"I think you should take the reins of the Children's Society Group, Simon. You need to be taking a more active role, and those charities will be the ones which boost your image with the public and the board. Please announce your intention today. Charles Spaeth will second."

"Yes, okay," was his reply.

"You'll need a secretary of your own, at least a part time secretary. Deborah, have Simon give you his requirements, and place an ad this afternoon."

They arrived at the hotel and as Simon stepped out of the car, as if on cue, his melancholy countenance was replaced by a cheerful mask. He exuded charm. He even appeared genuinely interested in the goings-on of the meeting, and by the end had been appointed to head the children's charities under the foundation's banner.

Deborah had not spent much time with Simon, and none of it had ever been alone. They sat now in her office while she wrote out his requirements for a secretary. She nervously approached the topic of gender. "I believe it would be most appropriate, look better, and help you achieve more if you hired a man."

"Yes, I agree. I don't want to give people a reason for more gossip. I can also avoid gold diggers trying to hook their claws into me."

Deborah was slightly taken aback. Did people think all female assistants were gold diggers? Did they think she was a gold digger? Did Jacob think that? Whatever the reason, Simon was willing to have a male assistant, and that satisfied Deborah. She moved on to the next topics of hours per week, education, responsibilities, and salary.

Simon didn't appear as forlorn as he had that morning, but he was also somewhat disconnected from the conversation. It was not unusual for him to be distant or snobbish. Yet after spending several hours with him, Deborah was beginning to wonder if his aloofness was really the result of sadness. She had never noticed sadness in him before. His voice more often boomed than not, and he always seemed to enjoy his circumstances. Maybe it was all just the role he was playing, the standards that were expected of him.

After placing the ad and arranging the best time to schedule interviews, the two went downstairs to have lunch. Oliver was in the dining room talking to his mother about Sarah's next school term. They were weighing the values and detriments of a boarding school over her current day school. Simon was suddenly the boisterous man Deborah had grown used to. "Ollie, old man, good to see you!" He walked over to the buffet and slapped his brother on the back, nearly knocking the glass from Oliver's hand.

"I'm fine, Simon. You look well." Oliver took a seat at the table. "We were just discussing Upton Academy for Sarah. Did you enjoy your time there? Do you think her education would be more complete if she went away to school or if she stayed at Highland?"

Highland Academy was a school for gifted children. In the case of Sarah and most of the other children who attended, Deborah understood gifted to mean wealthy. Deborah wanted to shout, "But she's only nine! How could you send her away?" Abruptly she realized she was staring at them, and tried to appear interested in the buffet instead.

Simon looked at his brother and mother, poured a bloody Mary, and said, "I loved Upton, but remember, we were twelve when we started there. The education is first class, though. To be honest, I don't think it matters much as long as she's in some prestigious place like Upton or Highland." He changed the subject to the regatta next week. "Ollie, will you be joining me? I'm sailing. I could use a good second."

The conversation continued and Deborah wondered if she had misjudged Simon. He might be a snob, and he certainly lacked no conceit, but perhaps he was not as narcissistic as he appeared.

DON'T JUDGE ME

"You look so in bloom lately Deborah," Catherine Copeland told her secretary. "May I guess that there is a man catching your interest?" She got the answer in Deborah's blush before any words came.

"There is someone. I've only dated him the once. I enjoyed it and I've been thinking of cooking dinner for him."

"Who is he?" Mrs. Copeland asked, leaning in closer like an excited teenager.

"Jacob Armel," Deborah answered, letting herself show the same excitement. "He made me a salad a few weeks ago. We had dinner at his pool. I haven't stopped thinking about him since. He's been flirting with me but we haven't had a chance to spend more time together. He is so nice!"

Mrs. Copeland straightened, then took Deborah's hand and looked her in the eye. "I do not think you should date that man. Please be careful."

Deborah pulled her hand from her employer's and sat up straight, considering a retort, but was not about to begin an argument with her boss. At the same time, she was an adult, and would date whomever she pleased. She couldn't grasp why Mrs. Copeland wouldn't trust her judgment.

Deborah scowled at her tiny kitchen and decided she could not cook dinner for Jacob here. She determined she would take him out to eat, but ventured that no place within her means would impress him. He dined at the finest restaurants more often than he ate at home. She would have to come up with another plan, something Jacob would never think of on his own. Then it came to her. Epsilon was doing a show in New Haven, and she would invite Jacob. That was certainly not something he normally did. Their music was probably different than his usual taste, and the experience would let him get a feel for the kind of things Deborah enjoyed. She could have walked over to the house to extend the invitation, but she called him instead. "Hi, Jacob. how are you?"

"I'm well." It sounded as if she had interrupted something.

"I'm sorry to disturb you. I was wondering if you wanted to head over to New Haven on Saturday and see a rock concert with me."

"You could never disturb me, Deborah. That sounds fun. I am busy at the moment, so I'll talk to you tomorrow. Have a good evening." Deborah heard a child's voice in the background and realized he must be entertaining his niece.

"Okay, thank you. Good night." The phone clicked. Deborah could not keep herself from smiling at the prospect of treating Jacob to the experience. Introducing him to Ash and the rest of the band would be icing on the cake.

She had been writing back and forth with Ash since New York and was happy to have such a good friend in him. She had gotten to know him like no one since Jackie. She had even told him the real reason she was not speaking to her family. She had told him the events of the birthday party all those years ago, of testifying against her father in court, and watching him deny every accusation.

Ash had told her about his relationship with God and how being in a rock band affected people's perceptions of him as a Christian. He wrote, *"I got fired from my first job as a music pastor because I have tattoos. But they knew about the tattoos when they hired me. They let me go when they heard I was in a band which performed in bars. My personal life, the good work I had done, did nothing to prove to them that I was a Christian. I left that job disillusioned. My music means a lot to me. But then, I met a pastor, Pastor Joe Carter. He had some tattoos. He listened to hard rock. He'd heard the band even though we hadn't made our first record yet, and he liked me. He happened to be looking for a music minister. He hired me and I've worked at that church ever since. But when some fans find out I'm Christian or when some Christians find out I'm in a band they judge me. I think it's made it easier not to care about pleasing people."* He talked about his family, his parents and his life growing up in Tennessee. He told her about his life. She thought she might know Ash as well as she knew Jackie, even though Jackie had been her friend since childhood. She could hardly wait to introduce Jacob to him.

TWO PRINCES

Jacob drove to New Haven in his red Jaguar sedan. He drove so fast that there were several times when Deborah caught herself holding tightly to her seat. Either he didn't notice her white knuckles or he chose not to acknowledge them, treating Deborah to stories about a wide range of things, from business ventures to Baroque music to Quebecois cuisine. She listened to his stories to distract herself from his driving, which she hoped was not as careless as it felt.

Handsome Dan's House, where Epsilon was performing, was a trendy little college pub decorated with bulldogs and various Yale athletic paraphernalia. The couple took a seat at a table behind the floor where most people would be standing for the show. Deborah saw Jim Ramirez by the bar and waved at him. He smiled broadly, waved back, and disappeared. His band was not playing that evening, so Deborah assumed he was there to see his friends.

After a few minutes, Ash came from

backstage to the table where Jacob and Deborah were sitting. "Deborah! Jim just told me you're here. What a surprise to see you!" He hugged Deborah, then held his hand out for Jacob. "I'm Asher. Deborah is a good friend of mine."

Jacob shook his hand and spoke formally, "Jacob Armel. Pleased to meet you." He then leaned in close to Deborah and put his arm around her. "Deborah is great, isn't she? I'm really happy she asked me out on a date to have an experience I haven't enjoyed before."

For a moment Ash looked disheartened, then recovered and smiled again. He sat down at the table with them. "Deborah, I have the pictures from New York." He pulled out his phone and together they looked through the photos, which brought back memories of a satisfying day. "Look at this one," Ash told her, "and the funny faces Jim, Andrea, and I are making! You, of course, look great in every one of these. I wish I was as photogenic."

Jacob remained aloof toward Ash and said, "I noticed that too, dear. You're not behaving inanely in any of these pictures."

Deborah sighed and said, "I want to be able to make faces and have a good time being silly. But I don't feel comfortable doing it. When I was a kid, I was super shy and very lonely. That made me gullible and it made me fodder for bullies. Trying to fit in with cliques got me tricked a few times. I did what I thought would help me conform, and I would end up being teased." What was it about Ash that made her share this kind of stuff?

Jacob replied, "Ah, well, you're grown up now, and much too lovely to lower yourself to make childish faces for photos."

Ash squeezed her hand, ignored the insult, and said, "Sorry you had experiences like that. You are lovely and loved." He blushed and looked at his watch. "I need to get backstage. The guys like to have a meeting before we go on."

Deborah was sure he had more time, since there were two other bands before Epsilon, but she didn't stop him.

With Ash gone, Jacob relaxed his stiffness and seemed to have a good time. Of course he never joined the others in screaming or dancing, and after the show he seemed very eager to leave the loud and crowded bar. When they were finally on the way back to the car, away from the noise of Handsome Dan's he laughed and playfully said, "Well, I would never have pegged you as a rocker chick."

"That is just one of the many aspects of who I am that make me an enigma worth untangling," she said flirtatiously.

"How do you know this Asher?" he asked, sounding serious.

Deborah described how they had met and what fast friends they had become.

Jacob had apparently not been very impressed with Ash. "To each his or her own. Asher acts a little young for his age. I hope he has a day job. Depending on rock music for one's income is never a sound plan."

Deborah was disappointed. She had

wanted them to be friends. Perhaps all they needed was to spend more time together and they would find some things they had in common. She let it go and changed the subject.

LOST IN PARADISE

The rain outside made Deborah's office feel cozy, as did the nice big cup of tea that warmed her while she wrote out Oliver's household checks and balanced his budget. She was consistently astounded by the amount of money he and Kelly spent each month, although compared to Mrs. Copeland's expenditures they looked positively frugal. The monthly upkeep of the house alone was more than Deborah had earned annually in her high school job, and that didn't include the clothes, jewelry, or other expenses required for their extravagant lifestyle. Deborah was not used to that kind of money, and had no desire to ever be comfortable with it. To her, an expensive pair of jeans cost fifty bucks. To Kelly Copeland and most of the other members of high society, if they stooped to wearing jeans, the price tag would need to read at least two hundred dollars.

The house line rang and Deborah picked it up. Ian was on the other end. "Miss Wade, have you seen Oliver? We've been looking for him for over two hours now."

"I'm sorry; I didn't even know he was

visiting. He likes the library, or maybe he's watching the rain from the terrace."

"No, he isn't anywhere that we've searched, and we have checked the entire house including the library more than once." He sounded concerned.

"Well," said Deborah, "I'm happy to help look for him. I'm sure he's fine." Deborah couldn't understand why Ian was so worried about an adult. Perhaps Oliver had simply gone home. "Have you called him?"

"We did, but we found his phone on the breakfast table. We're going to ask Irving, Tom, and their men to go look outside." His alarm was nearly palpable.

To pull Irving from house repairs and Tom from the landscaping to search for a grown man seemed extreme to Deborah. They knew him better than she did, though, and she realized they must be worried for some reason. She decided to put on a raincoat and search for him too.

Cumberland Manor was a very large estate with multiple buildings, extensive gardens, tennis courts, stables, more than one pool, and ample land. Deborah caught a glimpse of Irving as he headed to the stables for a horse in order to make the search faster. The rain was coming down harder, and Deborah began to fear that Oliver could be hurt somewhere if he had not come inside from the rain.

She felt as if she had been walking for ages by the time she reached the Labyrinth Gardens, a fantastical maze of hedges decorated with topiaries of fairies, goblins, and other storybook creatures. She took a breath, somewhat afraid to enter the elaborate garden, but there was a chance Oliver could be hurt inside.

Ten minutes later she found him wandering through the maze. He was not unconscious, but he looked afraid until he saw Deborah and gave her a casual looking smile. "Oh! Hi. I was just headed back."

"What are you doing out here in the rain? Everyone is looking for you!" Deborah could barely fathom that he was just taking a walk, or that he could be unconcerned or even unaware about the worry he had caused. How dare he? She buried her annoyance, remembered that he was an adult and she was the hired help, and decided he must have had his reasons. She would have to give him the benefit of the doubt.

"I needed some peace and thinking time, so I took a walk. I lost track of time. I can't find my phone. I'm sorry you were worried."

"Well, never mind; at least you're okay. Let's head back." She gave the very cold and very wet man the umbrella and coat she had brought with her in case she found him, and together they started back toward the house. She called Irving to let him know where they were and that they were safe. A minute later a golf cart driven by Tom pulled up to them, and they got in for the quick drive back to the house. Tom didn't say a word about the long search for Oliver. Then again, he rarely said much of anything.

Charlotte had started a fire in the parlor, and after Oliver had taken a hot shower and changed clothes, he sat by the fire under a blanket drinking a cup of warm milk. Deborah finished her work and joined him near the fire. The rain had been cold and she felt frozen to the core. Oliver looked far from warm himself. Deborah got herself a blanket and took a second one for the shivering man. As she handed it to him, she could feel the fever radiating off his skin. He looked at her to thank her but the glaze over his eyes alarmed her further.

Deborah called for Mrs. Copeland, who immediately told her to ring Dr. Baldwin. In an hour the doctor had arrived and was examining Oliver. "Young man," he told the thirty-something-year-old, "you know your immune system is compromised. You should not have been exposed to the elements for so long. I'm prescribing antibiotics and bedrest." He turned to Deborah. "If he does not improve, call me. If his fever goes above a hundred and one degrees, give him acetaminophen. He needs plenty of liquids, and he needs easy-to-take foods, plain soups, things of that manner."

Deborah was tasked with dropping Oliver off at his estate since she had to deliver him the new checks anyway. In the car on the short ride to his house, he remained quiet and shivering, although the heater was on. Before long the light sound of snoring came from the back seat. She called Franklin and asked him to help her take Oliver in from the car and straight to bed. It was alarming at how quickly the man had become seriously ill. What could have made him stay out in the rain, knowing how easily he got sick?

SECRETS

Deborah left Mrs. Copeland alone with her dress designer and went to Oliver's house to check on him. It had been a week since he had gotten ill. She had not realized how fragile his health was, but he had grown so thin and frail that perhaps it should not have been a surprise. Kelly was out shopping since Oliver had told her to choose a new necklace for her birthday party next week. Deborah supposed the party was more important to her than an ailing husband. Checking on Oliver's progress was only one of Deborah's motivations; she also wanted to find out what he thought of Jacob. It was clear Oliver had some opinion he had not shared, and curiosity had been steadily building in her. Whenever Jacob Armel was mentioned a look passed over his face. Deborah was sure Oliver didn't like him, and she wanted to understand what it was about Jacob that he found so distasteful. Deborah had spent long hours searching for flaws in the handsome and charming man and had always come up empty. The only thing she could think of was his seemingly unending parade of vapid girlfriends, but Deborah was sure he would put a rapid stop to that when the right woman came along.

She found Oliver in the living room next to a crackling fire. He looked better and no longer had the flush of fever. Her entry startled him, and he quickly closed the book on his lap, covering it with the pillow next to him. Deborah had already seen it: a kindergarten-level reader with a smiling panda on the cover. His face paled as he realized she had glimpsed the book. Both of them knew she wouldn't mistake it for one from Sarah's schoolwork.

Oliver uncovered the book and handed it to Deborah. "You know my secret now. The accident...I'm trying to teach myself to read again, but I haven't been successful. I'm trying to learn math again, too. I've made more progress on that front." His pallor was replaced with a blush of shame.

Deborah sat down. "You have no reason to be embarrassed. I had no idea the accident had caused that kind of injury. I'm sorry. But at least you're trying. Why not pay someone to help?"

"I don't think mother wants anyone to know. I am not exactly proud of being brain damaged. Kelly...she definitely doesn't want anyone to know. She hates me for this." Oliver sighed, and it seemed to Deborah as if he were grateful to have someone with whom he could share something he had been forced to keep to himself. He told her about the problems he'd had with his memory, emotions, and cognition since the accident. "It's why I got lost the other day. I couldn't find my way out of the maze. I couldn't remember how to get back to the house."

Deborah was amazed by his strength. So much made sense now, like why he didn't do his own budget and why he refused to text. It must have been misery to put up that kind of facade for so long. "I want to help you. We can do it secretly. It will be easier with some help."

"I'd like that," he said. "So, listen, I know you have a secret too. Now you know my secret. I get to hear yours. You never talk about your family. You change the subject every time they're mentioned. You don't have to tell me, but I'm completely vulnerable now. Why did you leave home? What happened?"

Now it was Deborah's turn to go pale. She swallowed, took a deep breath and forced herself to speak. "I was three years old when my parents left me with Uncle Eddie. He did something, something I couldn't remember for years, but it killed my spirit. I was ten when I saw him and had a hazy memory of dirty hands reaching down to me. Everything fell into place. I was sure he had molested me. Over time I knew he had. I was fifteen when I was brave enough to tell my mom. Do you know that instead of being shocked or even sad, she told me he had come on to her when she met him after she had married my dad? I knew she couldn't sympathize then. I had told her the most devastating thing ever to happen to me, and she turned it around and made it about herself. So I kept everything inside,

Uncle Eddie and all the other times too, the time when our neighbor Roger felt me up on my sixth birthday, the time when he made me touch his…"

She hesitated, stumbled over her words, held back her tears, and kept going. "He made me touch him when I was eight. I was fifteen when my high school P.E. teacher offered me a ride home and tried to kiss me when he dropped me off. There were so many times men saw me as a victim and used me. What did I do to deserve that? But the last straw came when I was seventeen years old. I saw my father fondling a little girl at a birthday party. I called the police, left home, testified against him and moved out of the state. I will never see my family again. I had a scholarship to Quinnipiac and an overnight bag. I never looked back." She took the tissue Oliver handed her and wiped the tears from her face.

He was crying too. "I am so sorry." He sat down next to her and took her hand in his, looking directly in her eyes. "I am so sorry."

"I feel so alone sometimes. I need a family." There was no holding back tears now.

"I'll be your family now, Deborah. I will be your brother. I will be for you what they should have been. No one will ever hurt you like that again."

"I would like that." Deborah felt a little naked, but somehow felt it was okay to trust Oliver with this dark part of herself.

Oliver glanced at his watch, jumped up, and hid the book in an ottoman. "Kelly will be home soon, and it's best not to make her angry," he said. "Maybe you shouldn't be here when she arrives."

Deborah yielded, and left feeling lighter than she had in years. She had a brother. Not since she had left Jackie's house all those years ago had she felt as if she had family to turn to. And she didn't think she could hope for a better brother than Oliver.

FANCY

Deborah took another look in the mirror before answering the door. She wore a deep blue spaghetti strap sheath-cut evening dress embellished with tiny sparkling stones in swirled patterns that made her think of Van Gogh's *Starry Night*. Her hair was swept up. She felt beautiful, almost too beautiful, as if she were a small child playing dress-up with a grown adult's things. She answered the door to see Jacob looking like a golden-haired Adonis in his tuxedo. They were going to the philharmonic to hear Sergei Prokofiev's *Romeo and Juliet*.

"Hello, lovely," he said, offering his arm.

Deborah picked up her wrap and bag, took his arm, and walked out to the waiting limo. The evening was warm, and her excitement at being on Jacob's arm made her even warmer. She knew she should have had something interesting or intelligent to say, given how hard she had worked to become culturally educated, but the only thing that came to her mind was, "I'm looking forward to hearing *Romeo and Juliet*. I saw the ballet once on a high school field trip. The music is beautiful."

Jacob smiled at her. "It is one of my favorites. Perhaps we can take in the New York City Ballet this season. I wasn't sure if you would enjoy it."

"Oh, yes!" she exclaimed. "I adore the ballet! When I was a child, my mother took me to the ballet twice a year, once at Christmas to see *The Nutcracker* and once during the season to see whatever they were performing." Despite everything she had told Oliver, she did have good memories of her family. Those memories made the falling-out so much more painful. She swallowed her pain and changed the subject. "Thank you for inviting me tonight."

"My pleasure," he answered. "I could not think of anyone else I would want to share this with."

The auditorium was alive with people dressed to the nines. The sounds of a thousand conversations floated over the melodies of the orchestra warming up. Jacob and Deborah were led to their seats just in time for the lights on the stage to go up, revealing the large touring orchestra. The music swelled and diminished and swelled again. The flow of it touched Deborah's heart, and she could sense her heart leaping as the music soared. She was certain she was feeling what Prokofiev had felt as he composed the poignant ballet. Jacob too seemed enthralled by the concert, yet he did not have to wipe the corners of his eyes.

During the intermission, people mingled in the lobby, drinking wine and talking. Jacob brought Deborah a glass of wine, then caught sight of Mrs. Templeton and Declan and led Deborah over to say hello. Mrs. Templeton smiled at the two of them but directed all her conversation toward Jacob. When the opportunity arose, Deborah asked Declan how he was enjoying the music.

He looked at her and coolly responded, "It's fine, but not my favorite." Then he turned to Jacob and said, "Couldn't you find a better date?"

Deborah blinked, stunned by his rudeness. How dare he? Jacob, though, countered quickly and quietly. "Declan, no person here could have a better companion this evening than I do. I am certain you did not mean to be so insulting." He then turned to Mrs. Templeton. "I hope you enjoy the rest of the performance. Have a good evening." He took Deborah's arm and walked away.

Deborah was unable to think of anything to say besides, "Thank you."

Anger tinged Jacob's words. "That man is so pompous. People let him get away with impertinence and arrogance because of his disability. It is ridiculous. What makes him or anybody better than anyone else?" He was clearly furious, but calmed himself. "I am sorry he spoke to you that way. I'm privileged to escort you tonight."

"Thank you," Deborah answered quietly. Did money and social position mean so much to these people? She had put up with a great deal of pretentiousness, but there were times when it shocked her to her core. She no longer felt elegant or beautiful. Now she felt as if she had been caught crashing a party she was not invited to.

Deborah arrived at work to find Catherine Copeland eating breakfast on the veranda and reading the paper. The lady of the manor looked up to watch her secretary come in, and motioned Deborah to sit down at the table, waiting with feigned patience as Deborah poured herself some juice. "I want to show you a photo from the symphony last night." She handed Deborah the paper, open to the social news.

Deborah took the pages from Mrs. Copeland and looked down to see, among other photos, one of her and Jacob walking arm in arm in the lobby. The caption read, *"Jacob Armel arrived to last night's performance of Prokofiev's Romeo and Juliet with an unnamed date. She is another in a long series of women the CEO of Grayson International has dated. This author wonders if he has plans to get serious with anyone any time soon."*

Deborah didn't know what to think. She knew he dated many women. Jacob had never claimed to be exclusive with her, and they had only been out a couple of times, but it hurt her just a little to think he might not be as serious as she hoped. She handed the paper back to Mrs. Copeland. "Well, it looks like I was a member of the glitterati for an evening."

"Deborah, I don't know how to make you understand, Jacob Armel is not the right man for you. He is not good enough for you. He has dated and hurt more than his share of women. He will get married one day, but I have to warn you, it will not be a love match. It will be someone his mother approves of. He is wealthy, but the largest chunk of his wealth is waiting to be inherited. If he marries someone she doesn't approve of, he will be disinherited. In fact, Martha Armel has already started telling him she has found him the right woman." She looked into Deborah's eyes. "He doesn't care who he marries as long as his mother approves and the girl is pretty."

Deborah was speechless for several moments. Her chest hurt with suppressed tears. She laughed, a short and false-sounding laugh. "I am just enjoying his company. We've been on a few dates, but I have no aspirations of marrying him. Really. I'm just having fun. I thought you knew me better than to think I cared about money." She stood up. "I have to finalize the invitations for the Harvest Festival fundraiser. Excuse me." Quickly, breathing heavily, she rushed up to her office.

Donna Campbell
WALKIN' ON SUNSHINE

Butterflies danced around Deborah's head, and she laughed, swinging her camera around and trying to snap a picture before they fluttered off into the bushes. A day of hiking was exactly what she needed. She felt at home in the peace and quiet of nature, and the solace of creation after all the intense emotions of late. So many competing thoughts filled her head about Jacob and how she had been treated at the symphony. She was also thinking about Oliver, and even worried for Simon. A day away from people was just what she needed to clear her head.

The sun shone down through the canopy of the tall trees, and she could almost feel the heaviness lifting off her. As a child Deborah had been a Christian and loved attending church, but after discovering her dad with Daisy, she had lost faith. Her dad had been a deacon in the church. He had been a pillar and everyone looked up to him. Since that terrible day she had not stepped foot in a church. Although Deborah still prayed in her own way, she no longer considered herself a Christian. Since she was unsure if anyone was listening, her prayers were more like meditation or contemplation, and that's what she was doing as she strolled lightheartedly through the woods.

Ash came to her mind. She had just gotten his most recent letter where he told her about some throat trouble. *"The doctor told me I had polyps on my vocal cords. I might have to quit Epsilon or lose my voice. I couldn't sing at all, and we had to cancel a couple of shows. I couldn't even lead worship at church. But my church family prayed for me. They are so encouraging. I'll go back to the doctor tomorrow to decide what to do. I need my voice."* He was a Christian and clearly found solace in the church. His words were so reassuring to her. He was not the hypocrite she had come to associate with church people; in fact, he was perhaps the most genuine person she had ever met.

Every time she contemplated her life, every time she started wondering what to do about Oliver or Simon or Jacob, Ash came to mind. She took that as some sort of sign from the universe to stop thinking about herself, and she said her first real prayer in years. "Help Ash. Heal him please. He's such a good man." That prayer had a comfortable and familiar feeling to it. She remembered her devout prayers as a child, and remembered the times when God had comforted her, when He had done things that she knew for sure had to be God.

When she was fifteen years old, she had missed the bus home and was faced with a long walk. Coach Baker drove up to her and offered her a ride home. She accepted since she had no desire to walk the four miles. He had been friendly, and when he stopped in front of her house, the middle aged man leaned and kissed her. It had terrified her. She had jumped out of the car and run inside her house, falling onto her bed and crying.

Eventually she had fallen asleep and had the most vivid dream she could ever remember having. In the dream her bed was her Bible, and as it let her sink into it, the Bible became God's arms. He was holding her, cradling her like a baby. He soothed her, kissed her softly on the forehead and said, *"I love you, my precious darling girl. I always will."*

Now, as she remembered that dream and the very tangible feeling of God's embrace, she began to cry. She didn't have to stifle her tears or worry about what anyone would think. She just cried. She cried for Ash, Oliver, and Simon. She cried for Declan Templeton, Kelly, and the other people who were lost in their own pretense. She cried for herself, too, for the little girl who lost herself to a predator, for the child who was bullied and silenced and oppressed. Maybe God was there. Maybe He did love her. Maybe He would be willing to forgive her for blaming Him for her father's evil.

Suddenly her phone rang. It was Ash.

"Hey, Deborah, I had to call you. You won't believe this. But I just left the doctor's office and she said that there is no evidence of polyps anywhere on my vocal cords or in my throat!"

"What? That's wonderful! I'm so happy for you!"

Ash went on to tell her about how he no longer had a sore throat, and when he went to talk to the doctor so they could discuss his options, she had examined him and declared him polyp free.

Deborah was thrilled for her friend. She had to wonder at the timing cf his call in relation to the timing of her prayer. Had it been coincidence? Or could it be more?

LIFE LOVE AND HOPE

Deborah arrived home that evening feeling tired but refreshed. Although her problems had not left her, they no longer weighed her down. Even all she had heard about Jacob wasn't bothering her. It was just gossip and couldn't be trusted. Jacob treated her like a princess or a precious jewel. What more did she need to know to understand his feelings were genuine? Her feelings for him were real. If he had ulterior motives, she was certain she would have sensed it.

After a quick shower to wash the sweat and dirt of the hike off her, Deborah decided to put on her bathing suit and head to the swimming pool. She swam laps and then moved to the hot tub. Sinking into the hot water gave her a delightful feeling as her remaining stress melted and left her. Closing her eyes and listening to the sounds of the world around her, Deborah knew she was happy.

"Well, fancy meeting you here!" came Jacob's melodious voice.

She opened her eyes to see the

breathtakingly handsome man walking toward her with a large smile. "Jacob! I'm so glad you're here." She scooted over on the bench to let him know he should sit with her.

Jacob pressed a button next to the tub and spoke to a servant in the house. "I need a pitcher of lemonade and two glasses. Thank you." He got into the tub, sat next to Deborah, and put his arm around her. "I hope your day was good."

"Yes, it was," she said, and leaned into him. It felt good to have his strength next to her and his arm around her. She could hear the steady beat of his heart with her head against his chest. They lingered that way, sipping lemonade, and watching the sun slip below the hills.

That evening in her little house she knew she was right about Jacob. She dismissed the social pages' hearsay, and decided that Mrs. Copeland just didn't like Jacob. Deborah did like Jacob, though; she liked him very much, and if he wanted to, he could marry her. He could give up the billions his inheritance promised and live on his millions. He might even be willing to be poor for her. She snuggled in her chair, opened her copy of *Sense and Sensibility*, and read until she fell asleep.

The morning alarm jolted her upright. She stretched out, surprised she had somehow slept all night in the chair, her book open to the pages that revealed Willoughby's true nature. Putting the book aside, she went to shower. The thought of going to church had crossed her mind, but she still held a great deal of anger toward the religious people who had let her father hide among them and had even protected him during the trial.

Instead she planned to go shopping in Belleshore and maybe visit the farmer's market. While making breakfast, she called Jackie and talked to her best friend about the tumultuous events of her recent life. As usual, the chat went on for hours, and so Jackie kept Deborah company over the speaker phone on the drive to Belleshore and in the shops as she browsed the sale racks.

"Trust your instincts. Jacob sounds like a good man. He obviously cares about you. Remember, he's the CEO of a huge corporation; I doubt he cares whether his mommy approves of his dates. You're right that it's all just rumors." Jackie sounded like a lawyer trying to persuade a jury of her client's innocence.

"You don't have to convince me. We're having dinner tonight at some fancy restaurant. He wouldn't keep asking me out if he didn't want to date me."

"What kind of newspaper reports gossip and photos of rich people on dates, anyway?"

"That's just Belle Cay for you. The paper here has a little real news, but it's mostly stock markets and gossip. That's what counts as news for rich people, I guess. Understanding who's who and who's doing what to whom helps them write up the guest list for their next gala. Speaking of which, I think I found a dress for tonight." Deborah took a photo and sent it to Jackie, who approved. With the conversation over, Deborah paid for her dress and continued her day of shopping.

NOWHERE MAN

The summer had turned to fall and Deborah and Jacob had been out at least once a week for the past several months. She and Mrs. Copeland chose not to discuss it very often. Working with Mrs. Copeland was very pleasant and the two had formed a nice professional rhythm. Her employer was out now having lunch with Elana Arcola. Deborah had just returned from renting a tent, tables, and chairs for the Children's Society Harvest Festival, which would be held at Cumberland. It would provide a fun time for the children while raising money to help place children in foster care. Now she was enjoying some free time.

Deborah and Oliver worked on the veranda, enjoying the weather while reading together. Oliver had not had a hard time reading. It was as if he only had to be reminded. In the past months he had moved from kindergarten-level books to third grade. He read to Deborah from a children's encyclopedia.

Simon came out to the veranda, a drink in

his hand. "Ollie, is mother here?" He glanced at the encyclopedia in Oliver's hands. "Hmm. Good for you."

Oliver was blushing a little. "She's at lunch in town."

"Have you had lunch yet? I'm famished." Simon sounded hopeful as he sat down at the table.

"You know, I'm hungry as well," Deborah put in. "Let's have lunch out here today." It surprised her that Simon had not said more to his older brother. He seemed to normally get joy from humiliating Oliver. The men agreed with her suggestion, and Deborah went inside to ask Charlotte to arrange lunch outside.

By the time Deborah and Charlotte returned with lunch, Simon seemed more his usual self, but now Deborah could see he was not the man she had judged him to be. She realized he was in pain, and he took it out on other people, but he also took it out on himself. Simon finished his drink and went inside for another. He talked about his new ventures with the foundation and suggested that Deborah collaborate with Arvin, his secretary, to sort out some details of the Children's Society fundraiser.

Deborah was not used to Simon pulling his weight, and was happy to lessen her work load. She enjoyed working with Arvin, an intelligent and thoughtful man from India who seemed to be undaunted by dealing with Simon's strong personality. At the end of their conversation, Simon was finishing the third drink he had had in her presence and was headed inside to get another. "Simon, do you really need another drink?" she asked.

He looked at her, eyes momentarily ablaze with fury. "Not that it is any of your business, Miss Wade, but this is water." He walked inside and poured another glass.

Oliver and Deborah glanced at one another. It was obvious Simon was lying; the smell and his slight clumsiness betrayed the truth. She made a note to speak to Mrs. Copeland about it.

That afternoon Arvin and Deborah were discussing the fundraiser. Deborah was impressed by how much work he and Simon had gotten done together. She handed all her notes, work, and receipts over to the competent man. Arvin was tall with dark hair, skin, and eyes. He was pleasant and kind, but not a pushover. In fact, his assertiveness stopped just shy of being too much. Deborah could tell it was this man who had kept his boss on track with all the work the foundation required.

Both of their phones rang at the same time. Deborah answered hers and stepped away so she could hear the caller. It was Mrs. Copeland, and she was speaking very quickly. "Simon has been in a car accident. We need to go to the hospital now. Call the car and meet me in the front." Deborah made the call and gathered her things.

Arvin's call had been from the hospital, reporting the same news. He and Deborah headed toward the waiting car to meet Mrs.

Copeland together. The lady of Cumberland Manor climbed into the car with uncharacteristic haste. "They just said he's in the emergency department and would not give me any further information." She was clearly shaken.

When the group arrived at Belle Cay Medical Center and found Simon, he was awake in a bed in the emergency department. Two policemen were talking to him. Deborah cold see no obvious injuries, but he looked pale. A nurse asked them to wait until he finished speaking to the police before entering his room.

Deborah went to the nurses' station. "Excuse me. We are here to see Simon Copeland, and I understand he is busy at the moment, but can we talk to his doctor?"

A lovely woman in blue scrubs came to Deborah and walked with her to the waiting group. "I'm Dr. Woods. I'm treating Mr. Copeland, and when he is done with the police, we can go in together. I'm sorry, but I can't tell you anything until I have his permission to speak to you. I will say there is nothing life threatening."

Mrs. Copeland shook the doctor's hand. "Thank you, doctor. That is a relief."

Dr. Woods had long red hair pulled into a neat ponytail, bright blue eyes, and fair clear skin. Her impish face and small stature contradicted her forceful presence. The police left the room, and the doctor led Mrs. Copeland, Arvin, and Deborah into Simon's room.

Simon looked relieved yet ashamed to see the group enter. He addressed his mother. "I'm okay. I'm sorry for scaring everyone. I'm a little banged up and they say I have a concussion, but I'm alright."

Catherine looked to the doctor and was reassured by a slight nod of acknowledgment. "Oh, thank goodness. Do you know what could have happened to you?" Her tone had abruptly turned reprimanding. "You were drinking, weren't you?"

He looked down. "Yes. I had been drinking. The police decided not to charge me. But...I'm sorry." Deborah had never seen him so remorseful, and was almost surprised that he was even capable of it.

"May I speak freely, Mr. Copeland?" asked Dr. Woods.

"Yes, go ahead, you can say anything. I have nothing to hide from them."

"Very well," she said. "He does have a concussion, and I would like to keep him overnight since his blood alcohol levels are still high. He also has bruised ribs and will be in quite a bit of pain, which I can manage safely here. However, the pain management will complicate the concussion." She turned and spoke to Simon. "A concussion is serious. It is a brain injury. I warn you, most people are not so lucky as to get away with concussions and bruised ribs after car accidents as serious as yours."

Simon remained unusually contrite. "Thank you."

Simon arranged with Arvin to gather a few personal items from home and clean clothes for the next day. Deborah and Arvin left together while Mrs. Copeland stayed behind with her son until Arvin returned. The two intentionally drove a route that would let them see the crash site. The car was still there, being loaded onto a wrecker as they passed. Simon's sports car had hit a tree when he didn't quite make a sharp turn on the winding county road. The car was mangled, and Deborah could not imagine how a person could have survived, much less come out conscious and whole. She took a breath and thanked God he was okay. Maybe this would be a catalyst for change.

Donna Campbell

REAPERS DANCE

The day of the Harvest Festival had arrived. The grounds near the Labyrinth Gardens had been transformed into a wonderland for the children, some of whom were already laughing and exploring. Deborah waited near the small stage for the Copelands to arrive as one so that Simon could officially open the festivities and thank the donors for their contributions.

Prior to getting on the golf carts which would carry them to the festival, Simon had proudly exhibited his "Thirty Days Sober" coin before placing it back in his pocket. Deborah noticed him reach into the pocket several times to feel the coin, as if he were drawing strength from it. Now she watched as Mrs. Copeland and Simon walked onto the stage arm in arm, with Oliver, Kelly, and Sarah behind them. The crowd erupted in applause as if the Copelands were the royal family of Belle Cay.

Simon stepped up to the microphone. "Thank you so much for coming today to share in giving this day of fun to the children of Belle Cay, and to the children of the Children's Society, whom we have assumed as our own. The donations you have made so far will go a long way to ensuring the Children's Society can meet the needs of the children in their care with healthy food, education, medical care, and hope for the future. Now have fun, spend money, and let's have a good time." He rang a bell which in turn signaled the lights, rides, and booths of the festival to power up. The grounds erupted into joyful activity as people scattered to the various amusements.

When Simon left the stage, he went directly to the waiting Denise Woods, the doctor who had treated him in the hospital. Deborah had been happily surprised to find out that the two had become friends and were on the way to becoming more than friends. Deborah went from booth to booth, wishing Jacob could have come, but he had cried off, saying he had important business.

Then came a familiar voice: "Deborah, I found you!"

Deborah turned around, thrilled to see Ash. He stood there like something out of a dream, his smile the most welcoming she could imagine. She rushed over to him and hugged him, trying not to squeal in joy. "Ash! What in the world are you doing here?"

"You wrote me about the festival and I decided to come and surprise you. The money is for a good cause, I have the time, and I've missed you." He took her hand. "Let's go into the maze," he said pointing toward the Labyrinth Gardens.

"Okay," she said, following his lead. "I am not a fan of mazes, but if you promise to protect me, we can go." She was suddenly happy Jacob hadn't come, and the thought bothered her. Why should she be glad for Jacob's absence? She knew at least part of the answer, that she hadn't liked the way it felt when Jacob had tried to get under Ash's skin the first time they had met. Ash had come so far to be at the festival, and she didn't want him to have to deal with Jacob's needling again.

The Labyrinth Gardens were quite beautiful. The whimsical topiaries and hedges were not frightening. Whether it was because Ash was with her or just because the garden was so well kept, Deborah did not feel the panic and claustrophobia a maze normally gave her. As they walked through the garden, Ash told Deborah about the various historical figures the topiaries and sculptures were supposed to represent. He told their stories with flair; his knowledge of literature was even bigger than hers, and she was an avid reader. Before long there were several children and two more adults walking through the garden with them, hooked on every word Ash said.

After exiting the maze the two walked over to a booth where people could churn butter and learn to make their own. Oliver and Kelly were there, watching Sarah vigorously shake a container of cream into butter. Deborah introduced Ash to them.

Kelly offered a limp hand and a smile to Ash, and even though she was not even slightly close to his height, managed to look down her nose at him as she said, "So pleased to meet you."

Oliver took Ash's hand in both of his. "I am very happy to meet you, Mr. Levine. I've heard so much about you. You're a good friend to Deborah. She means a lot to me, so I really appreciate that."

Kelly gave Oliver a confused look, and looked like she were about to speak, but thought better of it.

"Call me Ash, please," the musician told Oliver. "I've heard a lot of good about you as well."

Sarah bounded forward, holding out a plastic container with a small dollop of butter in it. "Look, daddy! Look what I made!"

Oliver took the jar, then kissed his daughter's head. "That is wonderful, sweetheart. Shall we buy some hot bread so we can enjoy this treat?"

She beamed, "Yes, daddy." They headed to the stall next door, which sold freshly baked bread.

The group spent the next couple of hours walking through the festival together. Anytime Sarah asked to play a game or enjoy a ride, Ash stepped in to join her. Before long, Sarah was walking along holding Ash's hand rather than Oliver's. Deborah couldn't help but take a little pleasure in the annoyance on Kelly's face.

Ash and Deborah were invited to dinner at Cumberland that evening with the whole family, which necessitated a change into nicer clothes for both of them. Dressed in her evening attire, she picked Ash up at his hotel and they drove to the manor together.

He was shocked at the grandeur of the stately home. "I could tell it was impressive from the grounds but nothing prepared me for being this close to it. How do they live in a place like this without getting lost?"

Deborah laughed. "I'm not sure. I've worked here for some time and I still get lost on occasion." They were greeted at the front door by Ian, who led them to the parlor where everyone else was already gathered.

Deborah introduced Ash to Denise, Simon, and Mrs. Copeland. Sarah was thrilled to see Ash again and left her father's side to spend more time with her new friend.

The evening passed quickly. The day's events were celebrated, and though the money had not yet been officially counted, the turnout promised that the festival had been a great success. Deborah really liked Denise; her strong personality was a perfect fit for Simon. Everyone seemed to like Ash, and Deborah felt the tension draining out of her shoulders as she realized no one was going to give Ash a hard time the way Jacob had. Though neither Kelly nor Mrs. Copeland were pleased by his tattoos or his membership in an up-and-coming rock band, Mrs. Copeland at least liked the idea that he was a music minister.

After dessert, as everyone was leaving, Mrs. Copeland caught Deborah's arm and pulled her aside. "This young man is wonderful! I am so glad you've moved on from

Jacob."

"Ash and I are just friends," said Deborah. "Jacob and I are still very much together."

"Well, we'll see," Catherine Copeland said with a wink and a smile. "A girl can hope."

WHY CAN'T WE BE FRIENDS

Ash came out of the hotel, carrying his overnight bag toward Jacob's car. Deborah thought Ash looked like an advertisement in a travel magazine. His long and curly dark hair, his leather jacket, and his bright smile made him look ready for a trip to some exotic locale rather than a quick lunch and a flight home to Nashville. He put his bag in the trunk and got into the back seat of Jacob's Jaguar. "Thank you for giving me a ride to the airport. It's nice not to have to take a taxi for such a long trip," he said to Jacob as he lightly touched Deborah's shoulder to greet her.

"I don't mind at all," said Jacob. "We can enjoy a casual lunch, you can have some more time with Deborah, and I can get to know you a little more." Jacob's choice for lunch was the Belle Cay Yacht Club, and the scenic drive let him show off the town as well as his own prosperity. Deborah couldn't blame him for loving his town and being proud of his life.

The yacht club was not crowded in the fall, but remained open year-round as it offered a wide array of sports in addition to boating. The outside seating area was closed until spring, but the indoor area offered a cozy atmosphere. The hostess led the trio to a comfortable table near a corner window with a view of the open water.

Deborah knew Ash had not expected Jacob to join them, but she was dating Jacob and was not going to exclude him from the plans. When she had told him that Ash had surprised her with a visit, and that she wanted to take him to lunch before dropping him off at the airport in Windsor Locks, Jacob had magnanimously offered to drive and buy lunch. She was very happy about that, because she thought of Ash as one of her closest friends and she wanted the man she loved to like him too.

Lunch went much more smoothly than their previous meeting at the concert. Jacob and Ash discovered a shared enjoyment of soccer and spent most of lunch discussing players, teams, and games Deborah knew nothing about. Ash did, however, get a chance to share some other news.

"Epsilon has signed with a record label. We got a deal for one record with an option for a follow-up depending on the debut's success. The label is going to take a lot of the work off our shoulders, especially when it comes to promoting and booking. I'll still be producing, though, and of course writing."

Deborah was ecstatic. "Ash! That's wonderful! Congratulations!" She reached across the table to hug him.

"There's more. The company isn't based in Nashville. I love Tennessee, but we decided as a band it would be best to move to New York City at least temporarily. It'll be easier with all the work we're putting in. And the best part is you and I will be able to spend some more time together." Ash said the last part almost sheepishly, but ended with a huge smile.

Jacob offered Ash a congratulatory handshake before pulling Deborah close to him in a sideways hug. "I'm so pleased for your success. I'm sure you'll be very busy most of the time, though. If you need help finding living arrangements, please let me know. I work out of Manhattan and have a second place there, and I can put you in touch with a very good real estate agent."

"That would be great. I think I want to make the move before Christmas. The sooner the better for me."

On the ride to the airport, Deborah was able to talk a little more to her friend. She listened raptly to his stories. She didn't share many of her own because most of them involved the Copelands, and she didn't feel right letting Jacob in on the intimacies she shared with Ash in her letters.

They arrived at Bradley International Airport after about an hour. Jacob stepped out of the car and got Ash's bag for him while he and Deborah said goodbye in a hug at the curb. She hated saying goodbye to him. Ash was so comfortable to be with, and he always made her feel good. She couldn't even imagine being anxious around him. Had they really been friends less than a year? It felt as if they'd known each other forever. Even Jackie said she felt as if she knew him from the long and frequent letters she and Deborah exchanged.

"Don't worry," said Ash, "I'll be moving to New York in about a month, and I will make sure we see each other." He hugged Deborah tightly then walked into the terminal.

On the ride home, Jacob and Deborah took the back roads rather than the highway. They drove through small towns and took in the beauty of the New England countryside, then stopped at a roadside market with an array of interesting fruits, vegetables, and jars. They walked from table to table tasting foods and looking at the offerings. Jacob picked up whatever Deborah said she liked and placed them in the basket he carried. Deborah pointed out a cute little homemade looking doll. "Would your niece like this?" she asked.

"My niece? I don't have a niece." He gave her a quizzical look, then understanding crossed his face. "Oh, my friend's daughter. I sometimes call her my niece. Yes, I think she would."

The crisp air sent a chill through Deborah. She hugged herself to keep warm. Jacob's strong arm wrapped around her and pulled her close. They walked as one person, and she no longer felt the cold wind.

Deborah breathed in deeply and reveled in the feeling of him by her side. She put her head against his chest and closed her eyes, trusting him to keep her safe. She opened her eyes in time to take a cup of hot cider from the woman who ran the little market. Jacob placed the basket next to the cash register and reached into his jacket for his wallet. Deborah missed his arm around her.

In the car Deborah looked the bags filled with apples, squashes, and jars of goodies. "Thank you, sweetheart." It felt good to call him that.

Jacob reached over and squeezed her hand. "I love you," he said.

Deborah's heart nearly stopped beating and for a moment she was afraid she hadn't heard him correctly. The smile on his face told her she had. Her heart began beating again and she wondered if it would burst from her chest with her glee. She almost squealed, but instead she squeezed his hand back and said, "I love you too."

LUKA

Thanksgiving was a week away, and Mrs. Copeland had asked Deborah to write letters to the foundation's various charities on behalf of the Copelands, wishing a happy holiday and including donations of meals. Simon had taken care of ensuring the children's charities were receiving dinners and volunteers to help serve them. He had been a changed man since the accident; it had been a catalyst for change exactly as Deborah hoped it might be. She was sure his new identity was only partly due to the AA meetings he attended. Most of his change was due to the influence of Denise Woods. He wanted to be a better person for her.

Deborah was working in the library because she loved to have the fire going on cold days. Oliver came in, with a limp even more pronounced than usual. He seemed surprised to see her, and slowed his gait in an attempt to hide the obvious pain of walking. "Hello, Deborah. How are you today?"

"I'm fine, but you are clearly not! What happened? You didn't drive here like that, did you?" she asked in alarm, heading over to help him to a chair.

He gave a half-felt false and pained laugh. "I tripped and fell down the stairs. I think I twisted my knee and probably bruised my arm as well. Kelly dropped me off. I'm in too much pain to drive."

She noted then that he was holding his arm close to his chest. "Oh my! You could really have hurt yourself. Let me look at it." It disgusted her that Kelly had merely dropped the injured man off at Cumberland rather than take him to the hospital. She rolled up his pants leg without waiting for permission.

His knee was bruised and swollen, and his lower leg had several contusions. She moved to his left arm, which was covered in bruises from wrist to shoulder. His right wrist was beginning to swell, too, and when Deborah saw it she got sick to her stomach. The bruise was the shape of a hand gripping his wrist. She rang the intercom into the kitchen and asked whoever was there to bring some ice packs. "Oliver, you need to go to the hospital and be sure you're okay."

"I'm fine. I'm embarrassed. What kind of man falls down the stairs?"

"I'm sure you are fine, but it's better to be safe than sorry. I'll go with you. Where's Kelly?" Deborah wasn't sure what she wanted the answer to be, but she hoped that wherever she was, she couldn't come to meet them at the hospital. Could Kelly have been strong enough to do this to her husband? The woman had been careless enough not to mind that he could need medical attention. Could she be ruthless enough to hurt someone like that? Deborah was sad to think she could. She knew Kelly had slapped Oliver at least once, and that when Kelly lost her temper she went from cold to furious in the blink of an eye. Deborah had wondered several times if the slap had not been the only time the woman had become violent.

"She's getting a massage."

"Oliver," she said looking him in the eye, "Did you trip and fall down the stairs or did Kelly have something to do with this?"

He looked away quickly. "What? No! Are you serious? Kelly is barely a hundred pounds. Kelly didn't do this. I tripped. That's all."

Charlotte brought ice packs and gave them to Deborah. She applied one to Oliver's knee and gave the other to him. He put it on his shoulder and winced, keeping his eyes averted. "I don't want to go to the hospital. Let's call Denise."

"She'll only tell you that you need x-rays and then make you go to the hospital. Come on," Deborah said, gathering her purse and keys. Oliver finally consented, and leaned on Deborah as she led him to her car.

There were no broken bones. Oliver's knee was badly sprained and his rotator cuff had been torn. A brace held his shoulder in place, and his knee was wrapped. He needed crutches but couldn't use them because of his arm, so he would have to rent a wheelchair for a few days. The doctor had asked questions about feeling safe and if anyone would hurt him before pointing out the hand-shaped bruise on Oliver's wrist. It became apparent to Deborah that the doctor was not going to let Oliver get away with non-answers.

"My wife tried to stop me from falling. She grabbed my wrist, but she wasn't strong enough to stop the fall." Oliver tried to explain how it had happened, but it didn't make any sense to the doctor, who could see more to the bruises than Deborah could.

"Did she fall after you?" the doctor asked incredulously. "At any rate, If the fall happened the way you describe, the bruise should be on your left wrist."

"Well, Dr. Burke, I don't know what to tell you. Maybe I described the fall wrong. It was happening very quickly, after all. She tried to stop me and couldn't, so I stopped myself as best I could." Oliver sounded angry. He never sounded angry, and Deborah thought it felt very out of place coming from the normally kind and placid man.

REARVIEW MIRROR

When Mrs. Copeland heard what had happened, she insisted that Oliver come back to Cumberland instead of his house. He was happy to rest in his mother's quiet home for a while. Although she wanted him to be taken upstairs to his old room and go to bed, Oliver had refused. He sat in a chair in the large living room, dozing sporadically from the effects of the strong pain pills the doctor had prescribed.

"Where is that girl?" Catherine asked, referring to Kelly, who had not been heard from since dropping Oliver off hours earlier.

"I haven't called her. She doesn't know I went to the ER. She's having a spa day," answered Oliver in a groggy voice.

"You ought to call her. She shouldn't be relaxing while you are suffering! How could she not see how badly you were injured?" Catherine put a throw blanket over her son, arranged a pillow under his knee, and plumped the cushion behind his back. "I'm going to an appointment, dear. Do you need anything?"

"Mmmm...no, thank you, Mother."

Deborah placed a carafe of water next to

Oliver. "Don't worry; I'm here. If he needs anything I can get it."

"Thank you, Deborah. I do appreciate you. I'll let Ian know you'll be here for dinner. Oliver, call your wife. Leave her a message that she and Sarah should come for dinner. You are welcome to recuperate here if you choose." Catherine Copeland left the room without waiting for a response.

Oliver answered her anyway. "I'll recuperate at home. Love you."

Deborah watched his breathing slow and grow regular. She picked up her copy of *The Princess Bride* and read. After twenty minutes or so, she noticed that Oliver was awake. "Can I get you anything?"

"No, thank you," he answered. "I'd better call Kelly." There was no answer, and Oliver left a message letting her know that she ought to come for dinner at Cumberland. He didn't mention his injuries.

Deborah was curious about what had really happened. She wanted to tell him to please stay at Cumberland, at least while he was going to require so much help with his knee and his shoulder out of commission. Instead, she waited for him to finish leaving the message before asking, "What really happened?" She knew that the pain medicine would make him less inhibited, which made her feel a little guilty, but she needed to know the truth.

Oliver looked up, still woozy from the medication, and sighed. "I forgot Kelly had an appointment. We were about to head downstairs. I asked her if she wanted to go out for lunch. She gets furious when I forget things. She began yelling saying things like, 'Do I look like I have time to go to lunch?' and telling me she was tired of me. She said I just didn't care about her. Then she hit me in the stomach. She kept yelling. I tried to apologize, but it didn't matter what I said; she wouldn't stop. Nothing stops her when she goes off like that. She kept hitting me. I was starting to walk down the stairs. She grabbed me and sort of pushed and screamed to hurry up. I fell. I tried to stop myself. She didn't even care. I was at the bottom of the stairs and she stepped over me. When I did manage to get up I apologized. I didn't mean to forget her spa day. I guess I asked her to drop me here because I knew I wanted to see you and mother, and I didn't want to be alone."

Unsurprised but still in disbelief, Deborah rested her chin on her hand, mostly to keep her mouth from falling open. To hear it was so much more than to suspect it. She thought maybe asking him while he was under the influence of an opioid was not fair. "Oliver, I'm sorry. I shouldn't have asked you right now. You're... you must be exhausted."

"No. I've wanted to tell someone for so long. I'm so ashamed. I know she doesn't mean it. I mean, it's hard for her. I'm not the man she married. She wants the old me, the better me back." He tried to reposition himself and winced with the pain.

Deborah shook her head. "That does not give her the right to use violence against you.

It's not like you asked to be this way. And your accident was not your fault."

"No, it wasn't, but it's not her fault either. Can you imagine how hard it is for her? I forget everything. I have to have Franklin remind me of every single social event or else they skip my mind. I forget if I ate. I forget entire conversations. Sometimes I forget how to do something simple like open a package of soap. It's really hard for her. She's stuck."

Deborah could barely believe her ears. "It's hard for you, too! I bet even harder than for her. She could be considerate and help you, but she's too busy being selfish. Instead of helping you get better, she punishes you for surviving a terrible accident. It is not okay for her to hit you!" Deborah hated the idea of someone suffering abuse. Oliver was so forgiving of Kelly, but Deborah was not so merciful. "This has to stop."

"I'll talk to her. She won't do it again, especially after she sees what happened this morning."

"She saw what she did to you," Deborah said heatedly. "She stepped over you and went to get a massage. She needs help. And Oliver, I know it is not my place, but I think you need to be away from her. I think you ought to leave."

Oliver looked down. "Can you get me something to eat? What time can I take another pill?"

"I put an alarm in your phone; it's not for another hour." She changed her tone, speaking gently. It was too much to ask him to confront the entire problem at once. "Would you like an apple or would you prefer a sandwich?"

Deborah left to get Oliver a snack and returned with an apple and some cheeses. "At least stay at Cumberland until your knee heals," she reasoned. "You need help. It will be much less upsetting for Kelly if she knows you are well taken care of here and she won't have to wait on you."

"Okay. I'll stay here until my knee is healed." He called home and had Franklin pack a bag for his stay.

AT LEAST THAT'S WHAT YOU SAID

Kelly and Sarah walked into Cumberland Manor's parlor before dinner and saw Oliver sitting in a wheelchair with immobilizers on his arm and leg. Kelly stood in the doorway with an annoyed look of disbelief on her face. Sarah rushed to her father, crying, "Oh, daddy! What happened? Are you sick again like when I was little?" She kissed him repeatedly, her tears wetting his shirt and face.

Oliver tried to contain the pain her touch caused him. "Sweetheart, I fell. I'll be fine very soon. Daddy is okay." He soothed his daughter, petting her hair with his good hand. "It's alright. I'm okay. There, there, it's not as bad as it looks. I only need to use the wheelchair for a few days. My leg is hurt, and since my arm is hurt too, I can't use crutches. Don't be afraid."

Sarah was pacified, but Kelly remained bothered. "Sarah, your father has a flair for the dramatic. He fell and now he wants the world to feel sorry for him."

Mrs. Copeland opened her arms for her

granddaughter but directed her words to Kelly. "That is quite enough. Oliver was seriously hurt this morning, and thank goodness he will be just fine. He will convalesce here. Now, let's go into dinner." She stood up and walked arm in arm with Sarah. Deborah pushed Oliver's wheelchair, and Kelly trailed behind as they made their way into the dining room.

After dinner, Sarah was sent into the media room to watch a movie and the adults gathered in the living room. Kelly sat as far from Oliver as she could, with her arms crossed and her back stiff. "Are you seriously blaming me for this?"

"Accidents happen, but sometimes they are helped along," answered Catherine. "I'm certain you did not intend to hurt Oliver so badly, but Kelly, you did hurt him. You let your anger cause some serious injuries, and he could have been killed. I have to wonder how many times you've let your frustration become anger. How often have you lost your temper with my son, or for that matter with my granddaughter?"

Kelly became even stiffer. "I would never ever hurt my daughter! How can you even accuse me of that?"

Oliver spoke. "You love her. I know you've never raised your voice to her, much less your hand. No one will suggest that you would ever harm her."

"But the fact is, Kelly, that intentionally or not, you did grievously injure Oliver." Mrs.

Copeland spoke with a little more compassion now as she took Oliver's feelings into account.

"It was an accident," Kelly answered coldly. "Oliver got me angry. We were fighting and he fell down the stairs. I didn't do this. Besides, he was walking just fine this morning. Do you think I would have dropped him off here if I thought he were hurt? I would have taken him to the hospital myself. This whole thing is an act for your benefit, Catherine."

Deborah cut in, not caring if she was out of line. "His injuries are real. His shoulder will require extensive therapy and possibly even surgery to repair it. His knee is sprained very badly and the damage couldn't be fully evaluated because of the swelling. I saw the x-rays and the MRI, and I spoke to the doctor myself. He is not faking this, Kelly."

"Kelly, you need a respite. I am going to offer that to you." Catherine Copeland spoke to Kelly as if the favor were for her benefit rather than Oliver's. "Oliver is staying at Cumberland Manor until he's back on his feet. If you'd like, Sarah can stay too. Even you are invited, if you should desire. I will ensure Oliver is completely taken care of, and you won't have to lift a finger. He needs more care right now than you may realize."

Kelly's fury threatened to crack her frozen exterior. "Neither Sarah nor I will be taking advantage of your hospitality. Oliver may stay as long he likes." She stood up, retrieved Sarah from the media room, and left without another word.

NOT YET

Deborah stood with Jacob at the front door of his house after a beautiful evening spent watching *The Nutcracker* performed in New York. Deborah had to admit she enjoyed certain perks of wealth, like private jets and box seats.

With his usual grace, Jacob leaned in and kissed her. His hand remained on her arm. "Come in," he told her, as he opened the door and tried to lead her inside.

"Jacob, I don't want to," Deborah said apologetically. She had told him months ago that she didn't want to have sex until she was married, and perhaps she had been naive in believing that he could simply accept her choice. "You've been so understanding. Maybe it isn't fair of me. I don't know. I am just not ready for this yet."

Jacob let his breath out slowly. "I've been very patient. I love you. You have to know that. If you love me, this is one way to show me."

Deborah wanted to cry. Fear rose up in her and became terror. "Please try to understand. I can't... I just can't." Images and emotions crowded her mind, and suddenly it was as if she were younger again, reliving what her uncle had done, reliving the birthday party where she had seen her dad doing the same. She collected herself, and when she could speak without crying, she said, "It's a long story, but I promised God that I would abstain until marriage, and even though I'm not religious, that promise means a lot to me."

"Do you think I could or would hurt you? You have nothing to be afraid of. I promise you. God made sex to celebrate love like ours. Come inside." He took a step inside the house.

Deborah was torn. She knew he loved her, and she didn't owe God anything. He had let her virginity be stolen from her before she'd had the ability to hold onto it. Yet she also knew she had the power now to do what she wanted, when she wanted to. It was her right to say no until she was ready to say yes. She was not ready nor was she willing to give herself away, but she didn't want to lose Jacob. "No. I'm sorry. Not yet. I love you, Jacob. Please wait for me."

He let go of her arm, kissed her cheek, and walked inside his house alone. When the door closed, Deborah walked around the manor to her little mother-in law house. She was shaking, afraid she had lost him and afraid she would never be ready to make love to anyone.

She undressed and got in the shower, letting the hot water run over her. Her uncle Eddie had abused her and wounded her as much as Kelly had injured Oliver. Even if she hands in delight, then pushed her father's wheelchair into the kitchen, where cookies, cakes, pies, puddings, and every imaginable sweet were being prepared.

"He is such a good father. She needs that affection," Deborah noted after the two were out of earshot.

"Yes, he is," Mrs. Copeland agreed. "Thank God Sarah has him. She certainly can't count on her mother for affection."

Deborah, Ian, Charlotte, and Mrs. Copeland walked into the library and went over the details of the party to ensure everything would be perfect. The Cumberland Manor Christmas party was one of the premier social events of Belle Cay, the glitziest party in a town that prided itself on glitzy parties. It would be a black tie affair attended by rich and important people from all over Connecticut. Deborah would be attending, not as Mrs. Copeland's secretary but as Jacob Armel's date. They had been out many times and were officially a couple, but attending a Cumberland affair as his date was special to Deborah. She would be another guest, not an employee.

As the meeting was coming to an end, Kelly entered the library. "Ian, please fetch my daughter."

"Good afternoon, Kelly," said Catherine. "Come inside. Would you join us for dinner?"

"No, thank you. Sarah has homework. I'm sure Oliver was too busy playing fun daddy to bother with it. Even if he did, I'll need to redo it. I am quite busy, trying to run a house alone right now." She did not come in, but waited stiffly near the door.

"Very well. It is an open invitation. I hope you will join us soon," answered her mother-in-law.

Deborah remained quiet; she had no idea what to say. The three women stayed mute as well for the next few minutes until Sarah's voice broke the silence. "Hello, mommy! Look, I decorated a cookie for you!"

Ian guided Oliver into the room behind his daughter. Kelly barely acknowledged the cookie and spoke to Oliver. "I supposed she didn't do any homework? You've been too busy playing with her to care about school." She didn't wait for a response, and Oliver didn't attempt to answer. Kelly turned to her daughter. "Come along, Sarah."

Oliver spoke up. "I would like Sarah to stay here this weekend."

Kelly's head snapped around toward Oliver, fury obvious in her eyes and barely controlled in her voice. "Are you a child? Do you think it is appropriate to discuss that right now, right here? You haven't given me much choice, have you? She will spend the weekend here, and I am sure that you will both come home Sunday evening." Kelly took her daughter's hand and walked swiftly out the front door.

FEELINGS

Simon sat at a small table in the corner of the restaurant, looking forlorn. Deborah was meeting with him to find out if he and Arvin needed any help with the Children's Society Christmas dinner and gifts. When she sat down across from the dejected man, a smile replaced his melancholy expression. "Deborah, thank you for meeting me here instead of at Cumberland. May I order you something?" he asked as the waiter approached.

"I'd like an English breakfast tea, please," she said to the waiter, then turned her attention to Simon. "How are you? Is everything alright?"

After a moment of thought Simon answered. "Denise and I are arguing. I want a drink really badly. I mean, I want a drink so badly I don't know if I can stand it."

"But you haven't had one. Right?"

"No. I'm not sure what is allowing me to keep from having a drink. Is it knowing that if I do, I'll disappoint Denise, or is it the disappointment I'll feel for myself? I've worked hard. It feels like every moment of every day is all about not drinking. If I give in now, I don't think I can recover. But being in a relationship is tough. I have to feel things, and I have to be honest about who I am. There's nothing to hide behind when she's looking at me. Who would want to hide from her? But if I can't hide from her, I can't hide from myself. I'm not sure there is anyone in me worth knowing or loving." He took a long sip from the club soda in front of him.

Deborah leaned forward in her seat, gathering her thoughts. "When I first met you, I didn't think much of you. I thought you were disingenuous and pretentious. But I didn't realize you were hiding behind a veil of alcohol. I didn't see you. As I got to know you, I began to see more of the real you. You are compassionate, more so than I ever imagined. You care deeply about people. Maybe that's why you turned to drinking, because you feel so deeply. You're sensitive and easily hurt, and you dislike hurting people. Those are good things, Simon. Please don't hide who you are, especially from Denise. She might be the person who can most easily hurt you, but I know she will do everything in her power not to. She needs your passion where she lacks it, and you need her iron will where you lack it." Deborah was surprised by her speech, but she knew she loved Simon just as if he were her blood brother. The Copelands had become her family.

Simon wiped a tear from his face with his napkin. "Thank you," he said quietly, as the waiter brought Deborah's tea. "Geoffrey," Simon said to him, "we would like two slices of the Christmas cookie cheesecake." He checked with Deborah to make sure his choice was acceptable, and she happily consented. The two moved on to the business of the Children's Society.

WINTER WONDERLAND

Deborah slowed to a halt in front of a full-length mirror in the hallway at Cumberland. Thankfully nobody was around to see her admiring herself. She had worn hundreds of very nice outfits during the past few years, but that night's was her favorite: a long glittering silver dress with spaghetti straps, matching heels, and drop diamond earrings. The earrings were not actually diamonds, but they were elegant and beautiful. Her dark hair was in an updo, her skin dusted with a shimmer. She felt like singing *"I Feel Pretty,"* and had to fight herself to keep from dancing around the way Sarah was. The younger girl was dressed in a red crushed velvet frock that echoed Kelly's dress, and she looked every bit the little princess from a Christmas story. One look made it obvious she felt every bit the princess as well.

Jacob and Deborah were dancing in the beautiful glow of Christmas lights to music from the band that had been hired for the party. Deborah was happy to see Simon and Denise also dancing and looking quite happy. Oliver and Kelly were seated at a table talking with another couple. Oliver's knee was healed but his arm remained in a sling. Over two hundred guests filled the manor, and as far as Deborah could tell, each one was having a good time. The party was everything Mrs. Copeland had said it would be. Enough work had gone into its planning.

Jacob's voice interrupted Deborah's reverie. "You're off work, Miss Wade."

Deborah laughed. "I'm sorry. It's just so beautiful! I'm so happy its going well."

"It is lovely, but you outshine everyone here. You shine brighter than every light and sparkle more vibrantly than all the glitter. How is it fair to the rest of the world that one woman should have so much beauty?" Jacob twirled her with a flourish as the band finished a song.

"Thank you," she said, blushing and quite speechless.

As the crowd applauded and a new song began, Deborah followed Jacob outside. He took two glasses of wine from a waiter and handed one to her. They stood in the cold, sipping their drinks and admiring the lights which covered every tree in sight. Then Jacob took the wine from Deborah's hand and placed it along with his own on a nearby table. "I once was a man who moved from woman to woman with ease," he said. "I enjoyed many women, but I never understood true happiness until I met you. I didn't know what beauty was until I saw you. I didn't know the meaning of joy until I came to know you. I didn't understand love until you loved me." He got down on one knee, took a small black velvet box from his jacket, opened it, and held it toward her. "Deborah, I love you as I never knew love existed. I cannot imagine a single day without you. Will you marry me?"

Deborah thought this must be a dream. It was too perfect to be real, but it was happening. "Yes, yes, absolutely yes!" She could say no more because she was crying big fat happy tears.

Jacob stood up, took Deborah's hand, and placed the diamond ring on her finger. He blotted her tears with his handkerchief, gently kissing her cheeks and then her lips. The people on the patio around them clapped and offered congratulations.

"Congratulations, Jacob and Deborah," said Oliver. "I'm really happy for you!"

Kelly took Deborah's hand, approved of the ring, and passed it on to Denise. "Oh, it's beautiful," Denise said. "I wish you every happiness."

"We already have more happiness than anyone deserves to have," Jacob said. He signaled a waiter, who brought a tray of champagne and two glasses of sparkling cider to the group.

Simon and Denise each took a cider and everyone else took a champagne. Simon raised his glass. "To the happy couple. Deborah, you have become a part of this family. Jacob, you are a man I look forward to knowing. May you both live a long and happy life together."

"Here, here" and "Cheers" rang out from

the crowd, and the friends all drank.

Catherine raised her glass. "I pray you are blessed beyond your hopes and dreams."

Once again they drank. Deborah was as happy as she had ever been. Her hopes and dreams were bigger now than she had ever dared to allow them to be. She wanted to remember each moment of this night, but it was being buried in a golden dreamy mist. She walked through the evening in a bubble of bliss.

Her mind was still fogged with delight when she arrived home that evening, far too excited to even think about sleep. She sat up and wrote a letter to Jackie, where she recounted each and every heavenly detail. She was about to write a similar letter to Ash, but decided she would prefer to tell him in person. An hour later she sat with her pen hovering over a letter that read, "Dear Mom." She couldn't think of what to write next. She was unsure if she even wanted to write and tell her parents. Then there was a knock on her door.

She opened the door to see Jacob in his tuxedo shirt, with his untied tie loose around his neck, looking even more handsome than he had when he was properly dressed. "I saw your lights were still on. I can't sleep. Maybe I'm too excited. May I come in?"

A pleasant warmth started in her abdomen and spread through her entire body. She wanted to invite him inside, but she was resolute, and closed her robe around her. "No, Jacob. I'm sorry. I'm ready to go to bed. Thank you for tonight. Thank you for being you, for loving me, and for understanding me." She wanted to kiss him but she didn't want to tempt him or herself.

The disappointed gorgeous man cupped her face, kissed her, and said goodnight. She closed the door and decided it was time for bed.

COLD

The next morning she sat with the same nearly blank page before her: "Dear Mom." Deborah put the stationery to the side and decided to call Asher. She wasn't sure why she should feel apprehensive about telling Ash, but the butterflies in her stomach told her she did. She dialed the phone, half-hoping he wouldn't answer, but he did.

"Well, hi, Deborah! How's my favorite socialite?" A glint of humor tinged his friendly voice.

"I'm really well, Ash. I have some great news. Jacob and I are engaged. He asked me last night and I said yes!"

For a moment there was silence, then the sound of Ash drawing in his breath. "Congratulations," he said without much enthusiasm. "I didn't realize you were so serious about him. Wow. Well, I'm really happy for you. Listen, um, you caught me in the middle of something. I need to let you go. Give my best wishes to Jacob."

Deborah was disappointed that she wouldn't be able to retell the details of the previous night with her friend. "Oh, I'm sorry.

Thanks. I'll talk to you soon. Bye."

"Goodbye," Ash said and hung up the phone.

Had his voice cracked a little? Was he upset for some reason? No, Deborah told herself, he was just busy. They would talk again soon.

By early afternoon Jacob and Deborah had finished posing for photos throughout Jacob's house and grounds. It had been a full blown photo shoot, complete with wardrobe changes and lighting. The couple looked through the digital copies to choose the right picture for the newspaper engagement announcement. Deborah picked a close-up taken by the fireplace in the living room. The announcement would appear the following day. She could barely believe she was engaged, but every time she looked down at her hand, the dazzling ring sparkled right back at her.

"We need to go visit my parents tonight and let them know," said Jacob.

Deborah realized she had not yet met Mr. and Mrs. Armel. The only thing she had ever heard about them was that they would disown Jacob if he married someone they disapproved of. Her stomach clenched at the idea of causing a rift between her fiancée and his family.

Jacob noticed the doubt and trepidation working their way across Deborah's face. He gently laughed and took her hand. "Don't worry. They are going to love you."

"How do you know?" she asked hopefully.

"I know they'll love you because I love you." He seemed to know exactly what she was thinking. "Stop worrying. Wear the blue dress, the one you wore in the trellis photos. I'm going to call and let them know we're coming. Let's leave in about an hour." He kissed her softly and went to make the call.

Early that evening the couple arrived at a luxurious penthouse in an exclusive high-rise in Manhattan. It was unlike any penthouse Deborah had ever imagined, more like a small mansion than a fancy apartment. The door was opened by the butler, Reginald, who led them through a room that reminded Deborah of a museum or palace, with furniture that she doubted anyone dared sit on, to a more comfortable though still luxuriously appointed room. There, sitting on a large chair as if it were her throne, was Mrs. Martha Armel. The regal woman remained seated, and Deborah had to approach her like a peasant approaching a queen. Deborah tried to resist the urge to curtsy, but gave a slight dip as she held out her hand. "Mrs. Armel, it is such a pleasure to meet you."

"Likewise, Miss Wade," she replied, with no hint of approval nor disapproval in her voice.

Jacob bent and kissed his mother's cheek, then sat down. Deborah sat on the couch next to Jacob, but left some room between them, worried she would feel judged about every move she made. It was important that this woman approve of her. She remembered the warning she was given, that if Jacob married against his mother's wishes, he would be disinherited. She wanted nothing to do with someone losing their family, especially because she knew what life without a family could be. Deborah had no idea what to say next and was about to comment on the décor of the Armel home when Jacob spoke.

"Where is father? I have some wonderful news to share with you."

Mrs. Armel's brows pinched together for a moment. "He should be down any moment." She turned to Deborah. "I've heard some very nice things about you, Miss Wade. Tell me, where do you come from? Where are your people?"

"Thank you, and call me Deborah, please. I grew up in Florida, but I don't have any family to speak of." She felt ashamed of her answer. She didn't consider it a lie, not exactly, but she was embarrassed that she could not answer with something that would make Mrs. Armel like her.

"I see. I am so sorry to hear that. You seem to have risen above your circumstances," Mrs. Armel answered, without giving Deborah any idea as to how she really felt.

Just then a handsome older man entered the room. Mr. William Armel looked very much like his son, but his full hair was snow white, his face distinguished with wrinkles, and his waist not quite as trim as Jacob's. "Welcome, Jacob." He sounded as if he were talking to a stranger and not his son. Then he turned to Deborah with a questioning look. Deborah knew very well that Mr. Armel knew who she was, but could see he required the etiquette of an introduction.

"Father, please meet Deborah Wade. Deborah, this is my father, William Armel." Jacob stood out of respect.

Deborah stood up, once again resisted the urge to curtsy, and held her hand out to the aristocratic gentleman. "It is so nice to meet you, Mr. Armel." Her stomach was in knots. How could she win them over? What was she supposed to do or say that would hide that she was not the high-class socialite they hoped she was?

Reginald entered the room. "Dinner is ready." He left, and Deborah walked beside Jacob, following his parents.

The dining room was just as opulent as everything else Deborah had seen in the home. She followed Jacob's lead, sitting opposite him and next to Mr. Armel. Mrs. Armel was seated at the head of the table. Reginald poured wine into their glasses, and another man served the dinner of squab. Deborah had never eaten squab before, and watched the others eat the tiny bird before she took a bite so that she wouldn't embarrass Jacob.

After several minutes of small talk, Jacob said, "Mother, father, I am very happy to tell you that I have asked Deborah to marry me, and happier still to tell you she has accepted my proposal." They spoke as if they held a script in their hands that Deborah was not privy to.

Mr. Armel raised his glass. "Congratulations. I wish you all happiness." He took a sip and then asked Reginald to bring champagne.

Mrs. Armel took a sip of her wine and said, "Deborah, I am very happy to have you as part of the family." Although their words were congratulatory, their tones were stoic. Deborah was happy to hear their words of approval, but wondered at the seemingly apathetic delivery. She wondered if there was any affection or emotion at all between them.

The evening progressed slowly. The Armels remained aloof and Deborah remained worried. By the end of the evening, Deborah had been invited to celebrate Christmas Eve with the family. She knew she would have to, and she knew that every Christmas from this one forward would be spent with them. She could only hope that as she got to know them more she would see more warmth and come to love them as she hoped to love a family.

I WANT TO TELL YOU

Deborah left another voicemail for Ash, her third in as many days. She hoped he was busy recording the new Epsilon album or otherwise taken up with work. At least, that's what she tried to tell herself, but deep down she knew he was avoiding her and she didn't want to think about why. She was hurt. She thought they were friends. He should be happy for her and celebrating with her, not jealous or slighted by her good fortune. "No," she said to herself, "he's just busy. He has so much going on that he just doesn't have the time to talk."

She turned to the still unwritten letter to her mother. "Dear Mom" were still the only words on the page. She took her pen and wrote, "I thought you might want to know." Then she signed it and put the letter along with the newspaper's engagement announcement in an envelope.

It seemed like a good idea get the letter to the post office before she changed her mind. Writing that sentence and sending the announcement was painful. It reminded her of the bitterness she felt toward the people who should have made her swell with love and joy.

How could they have hurt her the way they did? How could her mother have just let it happen? Why hadn't basic maternal concern kicked in when Deborah's uncle had done those things to her? Where had she been when her father had hurt however many girls he had hurt? Her parents didn't deserve to be a part of her life, but it also hurt that they weren't. It hurt even more that they didn't seem to care. Deborah never received a letter, a card, a phone call, or anything at all from them. They never asked Jackie how she was doing. They were fine with no longer having a daughter, and so Deborah would be fine without them. Besides, she had a new family in the Copelands, and was about to start her own family with Jacob.

The phone rang and interrupted Deborah's' mournful musing. It was Ash, and she quickly and expectantly answered. "Ash! I'm so glad you called! How are you? You must be swamped with work."

"I'm okay. I've been busy. We need to talk, but I don't think I can do it in person." He sounded somber and serious.

Deborah's heart sunk with a heavy weight. She didn't know what he would say but she knew she didn't want to hear it. "Okay, let's talk. Are you sure you're okay?"

"Listen, I just need to distance myself from you for a little while. I need to concentrate on my own life right now, my career and my personal life."

"Am I a distraction?" Deborah asked angrily. "I thought we were friends. By all means, if I'm bothering you, if I'm keeping you from being happy, then distance yourself."

He didn't say anything for several seconds. Deborah thought he was going to remain silent, and she had almost begun speaking again when he finally cut in. "Maybe you are a distraction, but not in a bad way. I can't explain it to you right now. I just can't be in your life. I want you and Jacob to be happy. You deserve the best. I hope you have found the best." His voice was slow and careful, as if he were barely controlling a tidal wave of emotion that threatened to break loose.

Deborah didn't understand, and he seemed not to be willing to offer an explanation. She didn't hide her emotions; she was in tears, and her voice wavered as she spoke through them. "Ash, why? You are the best friend I have here. I need you! You at least owe me a reason!" Then she was sobbing and no more words would come.

"Goodbye, Deborah. I wish you well." Ash hung up, but not before Deborah thought she heard him break into tears.

Deborah felt more alone than she ever had. She knew she had Jacob and the Copelands, but she didn't have Ash, and she couldn't call Jackie and tell her to come over and talk. She fell into her reading chair, curled up under her blanket, and cried until she was exhausted.

About an hour later a knock on the door startled Deborah from her grief. She got up, washed her face quickly, and answered the door to find her gorgeous fiancée smiling broadly. "Darling," he said, "I've made some lunch. Come on over and share it with me."

"You knew exactly what I needed." She was ferociously hungry. The sight of Jacob didn't erase her heartache for Ash, but it reminded her that she was not alone. She followed him over to his house where he had two bowls of steaming lobster bisque and garlic toast waiting.

The food was delicious, and Jacob's charm cheered Deborah a little. Remembering the pain she felt from her family and the fresh wound inflicted by Ash had made her feel as miserable as she could remember feeling in years. After lunch, Deborah followed Jacob to his den, a room much cozier than the living room, and they sat on the soft sofa beside the fire. Sentimental Christmas music played in the background, reminding Deborah of her losses. She cuddled closer to Jacob.

He leaned in and kissed her gently on the lips. Her hands went to his chest and she felt the strong beat of his heart. "I love you," she said.

He pulled her in closer to him. "I love you too. You will always be able to count on me." Jacob leaned in and kissed her firmly. He then tenderly kissed her eyes, her cheeks, and her lips, then moved to her neck.

Jacob was everything Deborah imagined she wanted. She was certain he would never abandon her. She yielded her neck to his mouth and welcomed his hands as they touched her back under her shirt. Then he

stood up and extended his hand to her.
    Deborah took his hand and followed him up the stairs.

Donna Campbell

BABY, IT'S COLD OUTSIDE

Christmas Eve at the Armels' home was not something Deborah was looking forward to, but she was determined to make the best of it. Since she was going to be an Armel, she would be a dutiful daughter, and she hoped that she would gain their favor, or at least get used to their cool demeanor. She walked in, leaning on Jacob for his emotional support. The penthouse looked as if it were the set of a play. Mr. and Mrs, Armel were perfectly dressed for their roles in the show. Deborah hoped she was dressed for the role of beloved daughter-in-law, and straightened her blouse where it was tucked into her skirt.

"Welcome Deborah, Jacob," said William as he took Deborah's hand and nodded at his son. It was more warmth than she expected, but it was not really a show of affection. He sounded as if he were just saying his lines and acting his part.

Martha also said the appropriate lines, and to Deborah they sounded just as unconvincing as her husband's. "Deborah, you look lovely." She offered her face to her son and he bent and kissed her.

Dinner was extravagant. There was enough food laid out on the sideboard for a whole restaurant. It too looked as if it were part of some theater production. Deborah only knew she didn't know her lines, and hoped her improvisational skills would be enough. Those skills were put to the test after dinner.

Martha Armel sat on her throne-like chair. Jacob and Deborah were seated on the couch. William went to the elaborately trimmed tree and retrieved a gift wrapped in gold paper for Jacob and a silver-wrapped box for Deborah. "Thank you; this is kind of you," Deborah said. She was surprised to receive a gift. It had been years since anyone had gotten her a Christmas present. Jacob handed his parents each a box topped with a card that read, "From Jacob and Deborah." Deborah knew about the gifts, a bell-shaped charm on a gold chain for his mother and a pair of cuff links for his father, but she'd had no part in choosing or buying them. He had just been thoughtful enough to add her name to the card.

She opened her box to reveal a beautiful gold watch. She was astounded. "I don't know what to say. Thank you. It's beautiful."

Mrs. Armel smiled and said, "You're welcome, Deborah dear. Wear it well." The plot of the play took a sudden turn with her next words. "Now, Deborah, our lawyers have prepared a pre-nuptial agreement. I understand you will want time to read it and have your lawyers go over it, but I promise you it is quite generous." She said these words airily, as if she were asking whether Deborah preferred crème brûlée or chocolate mousse.

But Deborah refused to be rattled. She wanted to tell everyone she was not after Jacob for his money, and she hoped Jacob knew it, too. She guessed that this was not his idea, but she didn't care. "Mrs. Armel, thank you. I will have my lawyers look at it, but knowing my Jacob it is very generous, and it will never become necessary. And knowing myself I will never give him a reason to divorce me. It was very kind of you to give me this tonight so that I'll have plenty of time to read it and consider it over the holidays."

Jacob was smiling and looked as if he might be trying not laugh. "Mother, I think my fiancée and I need to leave. We have a long drive home. Thank you both for a wonderful dinner." He kissed his mother and shook his father's hand. "Have a merry Christmas."

Deborah shook their hands, thanked them for the evening and followed Jacob out.

In the car, Jacob laughed. "You handled yourself beautifully, dear. You are my mother's equal. But I think you're much nicer." Then he leaned in for a kiss.

"Jacob, you know I'm not interested in your money. I'll sign whatever the agreement says because we'll never need it."

"I know you aren't after my money, and the pre-nup wasn't my idea. My parents insisted. It is quite standard though." He started the car and began the drive home.

She put her hand over his on the stick

shift. "I love you." Deborah cculdn't imagine losing him. "I would marry you no matter your bank account or your family." Then she smiled and added, "As long as you stay gorgeous." She lifted his hand and gave it a quick kiss.

MAYFLY

New Year's Eve was a day away. There would be a huge party at the Belle Cay Hotel, a masquerade ball. Deborah was more than excited for the ball and was finding it hard to concentrate on work, but that was the case with nearly everyone at Cumberland Manor. Catherine Copeland had left Deborah to her own devices, so she decided to go to the library and see if there were any book she might want to read.

The Cumberland library was filled with the classics as well as a variety of historical books and family records. Deborah looked through the carefully arranged fiction for a title that sounded interesting. She found *Shirley*, a novel by Charlotte Bronte that she had not yet read, and was just about to open the book when Oliver came in.

"Deborah, may I talk to you? I don't know what to do." His arm was still in a sling, but he was in therapy, and his strength and range of motion were improving.

"Of course! Is everything okay?" she asked

"Kelly hit me again, this time right on my shoulder. I think she might have undone some progress. I've been in awful pain. I made an appointment with Dr. Baldwin to make sure everything is okay. But I'm done. And I am not really sure what to do. I want to divorce Kelly. But if I'm not around for Kelly to hurt, she could turn to Sarah. I have to stay for her sake. I could go ahead and send her away to school, to Upton, but there are still summers, holidays... I can't leave her."

"Oliver, you can't stay in that violent situation. I think you're right; you need to leave Kelly. Fight for custody of Sarah. I can't imagine the courts wouldn't give you custody in the face of abuse."

"She won't agree to divorce me. She signed a pre-nup. She'll fight tooth and nail and that will mean dragging the Copeland name through the mud. That will mean people knowing that I let that woman beat me. It will be a scandal." He sounded defeated.

Deborah was hopeful that he would leave Kelly and escape her cruelty. She would be undeterred by his justifications for staying. "Your mother will help! She knows the best lawyers, lawyers who can handle all of this without stepping into court and without letting the public know."

"My mother detests Kelly, but she dislikes scandal even more. No matter how hard the lawyers work to keep secrets, the papers work harder to uncover them. She won't help. I would tear up the pre-nup and let Kelly walk away with everything I have, but Mother won't allow that either. The pre-nuptial was her idea. She is very protective of our name and our money. Besides, I don't think I have the strength for a battle, or the desire for one."

"You're wrong about your mother. She doesn't want you in that situation any more than you want to be in it. She is protective of your name and wealth, but I am sure she is more protective of her family. Give her a chance; talk to her. Besides, you're not fighting alone. You have us."

"Come with me," he said.

Deborah was ready to go with him, but instead remained seated. "You mother isn't home right now; she went to tea with Denise Woods. I think things with your brother and the good doctor may be moving along rather quickly. Let's wait for your mother together."

When Catherine Copeland came home, Oliver wasted no time in telling her he wanted to talk. He spoke without stopping; he had obviously gone over the speech a hundred times in his mind. "I cannot live this way anymore," he said, lifting his injured shoulder then cringing in pain as he paced back and forth across the library. "I have to find a way to divorce Kelly and keep Sarah away from her. I'm willing to suffer nearly anything rather than put my daughter in danger of living the way I have lived. I know the public may find out, but I can live with it. I am willing to be shamed in the eyes of people who don't know me if it means I can stop living in this shame. I know I may have to give her more money than she deserves, but I would rather be homeless and penniless than let

Kelly hurt Sarah. And I'm tired of being hurt. I'm tired of living with a woman who hates me and blames me for things no one is at fault for.

"I would like your help. I need your help, Mother. But I will do this with or without you. If it means giving her everything I have to send her away and get custody of Sarah, then that is what I will do. Please help me." He stopped pacing and looked at Catherine Copeland. "Please, I need your support."

Now it was Catherine's turn to make a speech. "Sit down, son." He did as she commanded. "Thank goodness you've finally gotten some sense. You could never be homeless, because you are my son and no matter where you live, your home is here. You will divorce that woman, and you will not give her a cent. If anyone should be ashamed, it is her. Robert Song is a very competent lawyer. He and his team will ensure a quiet divorce. And if it's not quiet, let the world know what a horrible woman she is. There's no question you will have full custody. By the end of it that woman will be begging you not to put her in prison for the rest of her life.

"I love you, Oliver. I want the best for you. Kelly doesn't deserve you. You are the most amazing and courageous man. You remind me so much of your father. You're too kind-hearted, and you believe the best about people, but there are many others who are not so kind. I will do everything in my power to protect you and my granddaughter. Come, let's call Mr. Song."

Donna Campbell

THE MASQUERADE BALL

NINE O'CLOCK

Deborah and Jacob walked arm in arm into the elegantly decorated ballroom. People were dressed in their most splendid evening attire, all wearing or carrying stylish masks, some of which were covered in jewels. Deborah wore a long purple gown designed to look like a seventeenth-century noble. Her mask was a deep purple with feathers at the edge and rhinestones underlining the eyes. Jacob also wore purple; his mask was not as embellished as Deborah's, being simple purple satin with gold threading outlining it. Deborah thought he cut an impressive figure in the outfit.

Music played as couples in sophisticated outfits and beautiful masks danced, stood talking in groups, or walked the room. There was a lot to take in, from the parlor games to the food and drink offerings to the trimmings. Deborah felt as if she were in a Jane Austen novel, attending a ball with the Dashwoods or the Bennets. Jacob and Deborah walked straight out to the dance floor and danced to the lively music. Deborah wondered if she had ever been so happy. She was at an amazing party on New Year's Eve with a man she loved completely. She was completely devoted to Jacob, and felt as if she were in heaven.

Jacob and Deborah found Oliver and Kelly, both obviously unhappy beneath their disguises. Oliver was talking to his wife. "You didn't have to come tonight. We didn't have to come. Why did you insist if you were going to be so miserable?"

"You may not care about your reputation, but I do. You are not going through with this." She sneered at him and her very pretty face looked quite unsightly.

"Kelly," Oliver began, and it was clear from his tone that he would tolerate no dissent. "Go get a drink, go dance with someone, or go home. I don't care where you go. Just go away from me."

She turned on her heel and huffed away, pushing Deborah aside as she passed.

Deborah resisted the urge to excuse herself to Kelly. Instead she spoke to Oliver. "I'm sorry we interrupted your conversation."

"Don't be sorry. I told her this morning that Sarah and I were moving to Cumberland and that I was divorcing her. She refused to believe it. When I had our things moved over, she threw a temper tantrum. Suddenly she was sorry and begged me for another chance. I said no, although I did concede to coming here with her tonight. But I won't change my mind about the divorce."

"Good for you, Oliver." Jacob shook his

hand in a congratulatory manner.

"Candice Lowery is here," said Oliver. "I'm worried that Kelly might talk to her and get a lot of lies in the gossip column."

"Who is she?" asked Deborah.

Jacob answered her, "She is the reporter for the Belle Cay Star Newspaper. She takes rumors and reports them as news. The glitterati eat it up; they love their social pages." He used air quotes over the words social pages. "Gossip is just an excuse for them to judge each other and think they're better than the next guy." He said it with disgust in his voice.

Oliver agreed. "It's true they'll gossip over anything. But I've seen her check her facts. When she reported about the accident, she had heard rumors that I was brain-dead, but didn't write that. Somehow she managed to get her hands on my medical records, even though I didn't grant permission for them to be released, and she didn't print anything that wasn't in the records."

Deborah spoke up. "Do you think Kelly gave her those records? She loves attention, and being the grieving wife of a gravely injured man would do that for her."

Oliver looked as if he had not thought of that before. "It wouldn't surprise me. She is not who I thought she was when I married her. I wish I could have seen the real Kelly before we walked down the aisle. If I could turn back the calendar..."

"If you could turn back time," said Deborah, "you wouldn't have Sarah."

"True, and your Sarah is a lovely little thing," said Jacob. "What else might you have missed out on if you'd never married Kelly?"

"I'm glad to have Sarah. But she is the only good thing that came from our union," said Oliver with a touch of bitterness.

TEN O'CLOCK

Deborah was enjoying herself, and she could barely wait to tell Jackie and Ash about this evening. Then she remembered that she wouldn't be sharing the excitement of the night with Ash. He had abandoned her. Her heart ached for him. When she had spoken to Jackie, her friend had been just as perplexed as she had been. Jackie had offered her comfort, but Ash had broken her heart and she wasn't sure if she would feel consolation anytime soon. Even sleeping with Jacob, which should have been a reassurance of his love, had not really done that for Deborah. Instead she felt ashamed that she had broken the vow she had made to herself, and resentful that Jacob had kept wanting it even though he knew her feelings. She lied and told herself that being engaged was the same as being married, but even she didn't believe her own deception.

She was sharing a dance with Simon and Jacob was dancing with Denise. Simon had changed so much since he had started dating the pretty and tough doctor. Deborah was sure she could not date a person so new to sobriety, but Denise took it on with a fierceness that fortified Simon. Deborah hoped she and Denise might become good friends, and she certainly felt like she needed another friend. With Ash, Deborah had felt he was all she needed and everyone else was frosting on the cake.

Deborah told herself that Jacob was truly all she needed in the world, and a temporary salve covered her aching heart and soothed her. A husband was supposed to be her other half, her completion, right? It was Jacob who was her soulmate, not Ash. It was Jacob who should be her best friend, not Ash.

"Deb, where are you?" asked Simon.

Deborah laughed, "I'm sorry, my mind is on a friend. Do you remember Asher Levine?"

"Of course, yes. How is he?"

"Well," said Deborah, "I'm not sure. I think there's something going on with him. But he asked me to give him some distance. I thought we were friends, but now I'm not sure."

Simon looked at Deborah with a touch of disbelief. "I think he thought you were more than friends."

Now it was Deborah's turn to be incredulous. "What? No! He never thought that. No. He only thought of me as a friend." She was beginning to doubt her own instincts. "He only believed we were friends, and besides, he obviously didn't feel as deeply as I felt for him. He dropped me."

"He is staying away for a reason, and if I gambled, I would bet that it's a broken heart,"

Simon said lightheartedly.

"No, I never led him on. He met Jacob. He even liked him."

"Did he know you were serious? You and Jake moved pretty quickly from first date to committed relationship."

"He knew," she answered, but she couldn't help wondering whether Ash understood who Jacob was. "Do you really think we moved too fast?"

"I said, fast, not too fast. And yes, Deb, I do think you moved fast. But who am I to judge? I am fighting my desire to move to the next level with Denise. I am trying hard to make sure that any move I make will not mess with staying sober. But in my heart, I already know I want to marry her."

"Follow your heart, Simon." The song ended and the two couples returned to their original partners.

Candice Lowery, the reporter, was headed toward Jacob and Deborah. Jacob quickly ushered Deborah off the floor and to the terrace. "Come on, I need some fresh air," he said.

Once on the terrace Deborah said, "She probably just wanted to find out about any wedding details. We could tell her we haven't finalized the plans yet."

"Our lives are not her business," Jacob said in a resolute tone. "Besides, I want to spend some private time with you tonight. I want to take in your beauty and breathe in your scent."

Deborah wrapped her arms around Jacob,

leaned against his chest and listened to what had become her favorite sound, the beating of his heart.

ELEVEN O'CLOCK

The tables at the ball overflowed with delectable foods, treats, and desserts. Deborah chose a chocolate-covered strawberry nearly as large as an apple. She was enjoying the delicious fruit when she caught sight of Kelly huddled close to another woman, looking straight at her. It was obvious the two were gossiping about her and that whatever they said it was malicious. She began to walk over to them in order to confront them, but then she saw Oliver and knew that she could not do or say anything that would make things harder for him. Whatever the spiteful women were saying was only gossip, and Deborah was sure it couldn't hurt her.

Moments later Candice Lowery approached the women, and they seemed to swallow her up into their huddle. The three looked at Deborah. Candice seemed about to invite Deborah to join them, but Deborah turned away, took her strawberry, and found Jacob by a table filled with savory delights. "Hello, sweetheart," she said as she reached up and kissed his cheek. "Oh, these look delicious." She took a toast point with caviar.

"Hi, gorgeous." Jacob returned her kiss.

His plate had a variety of foods on it, and he took a small cube of white cheese with something black on top of it and placed it in her mouth. "Try this cheddar and truffle."

"Mmm." It was really delicious. Deborah found the cubes on the table and put one on her own plate and another on Jacob's.

They joined Simon, Denise, and Oliver who were also enjoying the party fare. It didn't surprise Deborah that Denise had somehow managed to create quite the healthy plate of food for herself, even amongst the many rich dishes. Denise was very health conscious and had influenced Simon to live that way as well.

Denise finished carrot straws wrapped in seaweed and said, "That reporter certainly is making the rounds. I don't recall the reporters from the previous New Year's parties being so ever-present. It's normally just pictures and captions, but she looks like she's getting enough information for an entire article."

"I thought the same thing," said Simon.

Jacob swallowed his escargot and said, "I think she's digging up dirt on Kelly and Oliver. Let's support Oliver by refusing to speak to her. Please, let's not indulge her."

"No, of course not," said Deborah.

Oliver smiled. "That's really thoughtful of you all. I'm lucky to have you."

The conversation moved on to hopes for the New Year. Deborah's heart was full with the expectations of a new life as a married woman.

Oliver was hopeful for the new life of freedom from Kelly's oppression and the prospect of being a single father. "I think I will let her have the house. Sarah might enjoy living at Cumberland, and I can build us a new place, without any connection to Kelly. It's not going to be amicable, but I can try to make it as easy as possible for Sarah's sake. It might improve the situation for Kelly if she has the house. She's the one who chose it and decorated it. She loves that house."

"You are much nicer than I would be," said Jacob.

"Here here!" said Simon as he lifted his sparkling water. "To Oliver, to the New Year, and to new lives filled with good things."

Everyone lifted their glasses and joined in his sentiments.

Jacob drank his wine and suddenly took Deborah's arm, "Come on; let's dance" He didn't wait for her response as he walked her to the dance floor.

"Why do you want to dance right now at this second?" Asked Deborah happily following him to the dance floor.

"I want to relish this time with you. These are the last minutes of this year. Our lives are about to change. I want to savor every moment."

A slow song was beginning, and Deborah was happy to share the romantic dance with Jacob. He was unafraid of showing her affection anytime. In that way he was very unlike his parents, and she wondered where he had learned to be so different from them. She glanced back at her friends and saw Candice talking to them. Whatever the reporter had said had apparently shocked them. Oliver looked pale. Denise's mouth formed the word "no" and Simon hugged her with fervor. Deborah didn't turn back to join them, though. She would find out soon enough. Now she just wanted to be with Jacob.

MIDNIGHT

Deborah and Jacob held each other closely, swaying more than dancing to the love song. She was blissfully happy. The band ended the song and Mayor Nelson took the microphone. "Ladies and gentlemen, the new year is almost here. Ten, nine, eight, seven, six, five, four, three, two, one; happy new year!" The room exploded with applause, cheers, and laughter. Around them everyone was removing their masks. Deborah took hers off and joyfully met Jacob's lips with her own. Let the new year begin, she thought.

They finished their kiss and Deborah saw that Jacob had not yet taken off his mask. His hand was frozen in mid-air. She reached up and took the mask off his face for him. His panicked eyes darted to the left and Deborah saw what had startled him. Candice Lowery walked up to them holding a small voice recorder out to them. "Mr. Armel, I'd like to talk to you about the allegations being made against you."

"What? What allegations?" asked Deborah.

"No comment!" said Jacob as he walked away pulling a stunned Deborah behind him.

But Candice stayed with them. "Miss Wade, will you still marry Mr. Armel in the light of all these charges?"

"What are you talking about?" asked Deborah, trying to stop Jacob so she could confront the reporter.

"No comment," insisted Jacob, still pulling her by the arm. "Deborah, stop talking to her!"

Candice Lowery was undeterred. "Your fiancée has been charged with possession of child pornography and child molestation. Did you know about his activities? Did you participate?"

"No!" Deborah screamed. "No, no, no..." She couldn't say anything else. She couldn't think. The room spun and went white as she collapsed to the floor. She tried to make the room come back into focus but it wouldn't.

The next thing she knew was Simon's voice. "Shh, don't talk, Deb. Just close your eyes." Simon had scooped her into his arms and was carrying her outside. He laid her down on his jacket.

Denise was beside her now, checking her. Deborah tried to speak, but she could barely breathe. Denise's voice cut through the haze. "Simon, go get my bag and all our coats. Oliver, call for your car. Deborah, relax. Just breathe."

Deborah concentrated on breathing as Denise encouraged her. "Good in, yes out. Good in and now out, that's better. Okay, I'm going to give you something to relax you now." She felt a slight pinch. Then she was back in Simon's arms.

She heard Oliver's voice, "Jacob, not now. Go home." And she drifted off to sleep, dreaming of uncles, P.E teachers, and children's birthday parties.

Donna Campbell

PART TWO

BROKEN

Deborah woke up in a strange bedroom and at first couldn't remember why she might be there. Soon enough the previous night came back to her. She was wearing a nightgown she didn't recognize and lying in a soft bed in a large bedroom decorated with red and gold. She realized she must be at Cumberland Manor, and closed her eyes in the hope of escaping life and falling asleep once again. Her mind was racing too fast for that to happen, though. Could Jacob have really done something so horrible? No, it was impossible. She would have known! She would have sensed something. She buried herself deeper under the lush comforter and cried.

A gentle, almost hesitant knock came on the door. "Miss Wade?" said a soft voice.

"Come in," said Deborah as she wiped the tears from her face and sat up.

Maria, one of the housemaids, opened the door. She carried a tray with a pot of tea and a plate of toast and fruit, setting it up for Deborah as she spoke. "Miss Wade, the police called this morning and they'd like to speak with you today. Mrs. Copeland invited them to come here. She felt it would be easier for you that way. They'll be here in two hours."

"Thank you, Maria." Everything was happening without Deborah's consent, input, or control, but she didn't have the energy to put forth any effort or care. She looked at the tray and poured herself a cup of tea even though her stomach was roiling. "I don't have any clothes here."

"If you give Mr. Copeland your keys, he, Tom, and Irving will go to your house and pack your things for you. Dr. Woods suggested you rest for a few days, and Mrs. Copeland wants you to rest here."

Deborah agreed. She couldn't go back to her little house right now. She couldn't imagine facing Jacob with all this uncertainty.

She drank the tea and picked up the newspaper to try and stop her spinning mind. But it only spun faster when she got to page four and saw the pictures and headline. The headline read, "Jacob Armel Accused of Child Molestation and Child Pornography. Fiancée Plays Dumb, Denies any Knowledge." There was a photo of her walking arm in arm with Jacob, then one of him with his hand out toward the camera and a look of hate twisting his face. There was another of Simon carrying her out of the ball. She sat and stared at the page for some time, then read the article even though she knew she shouldn't. She grew more and more hurt with every unkind word quoted by the party's attendees. Many said they had suspected Jacob. Some claimed to have known.

Masquerade

The reporter had not asked why they didn't do something about their suspicions, hadn't asked why they let children continue to be abused if they were so sure it was happening. Nor had she asked how Deborah could have been ignorant to it, if the rest of the town was not. There were no quotes in support of either her or Jacob. She read the article again and again, unable to put it down. If this were true, how had she remained so blind?

As she finished her tea, Maria brought in her suitcase. She saw the paper in Deborah's hand and the pallor of her face. "Oh! I wasn't thinking! I am so sorry." She took the paper away, finally freeing Deborah from the article's grip.

Deborah took a long hot shower and tried not to think about Jacob or her inability to call Ash. Ash would have been able to calm her and tell her logically why Jacob could not be a child molester, but Ash wasn't available to her now. She couldn't bring herself to talk to Jacob just yet, wasn't sure what to think about him. She got dressed in a pair of yoga pants and a sweatshirt, not caring how sloppy she looked.

Downstairs she met Catherine, Simon, and Denise in the sitting room. Oliver was out with Sarah, so that the child wouldn't be exposed to the terrible reasons for the police visit. "Let's move to the library," suggested Catherine. "You'll be more comfortable there and we can light a fire."

Deborah compliantly followed her into the

library, feeling emotionally drained and not up to even the simplest decisions. She sat in a chair close to the fireplace, and Denise brought her a comfortable blanket. No one bothered to make small talk. They didn't ask her questions nor require any conversation or answers from her. They were simply there with her. Minutes later Maria, one of the few servants working on New Year's Day, entered the room, followed by Mr. Song. The lawyer, a handsome and muscular Asian man, wore a tailored suit and designer shoes. He sat in a seat near but just behind Deborah.

"Miss Wade," he said, "I don't suspect you need a lawyer, but I will be here to support you and ensure your rights are being upheld."

"Thank you," she said. She wondered how she could be in this position, about to speak to the police, with a lawyer in her corner. How could she be engaged to a suspected child molester? She looked down at her beautiful ring and began quietly crying again. A cup of chamomile tea appeared next to her. She assumed the thoughtful Maria had been busy at work, and drank some of the steaming sweet brew.

Finally the police arrived and sat in chairs opposite Deborah. They requested that everyone except Robert Song leave the room. Catherine gave Deborah's hand a squeeze and led Simon and Denise into the sitting room.

There were two detectives, an olive skinned woman with long dark curly hair and big beautiful eyes and a tall African-American man with a Caribbean accent that sounded out of place in the Connecticut winter. The woman introduced herself and her partner to Deborah. "Hello, Miss Wade; I am Detective Ruiz and this is Detective Robinson. Thank you for agreeing to meet with us today. I am sure this isn't how you hoped to begin your New Year."

"How can I help you?" asked Deborah.

Detective Ruiz opened a briefcase and removed a folder. She handed the folder to Deborah. "These are some of the pictures we found on Mr. Armel's computer. We've printed them out. Do you recognize any of these children?"

Deborah held the folder in her shaking hands, afraid to see what the detectives told her she would find. Finally she opened it and looked through picture after picture of little girls in various stages of undress and assorted positions. Some had tears running down their faces. Some looked dazed. None looked willing or happy. "Oh, these are…" Deborah began to gag. "I think I'm going to be sick!"

Mr. Song rushed to her side. "Let me help her to the bathroom; she will be right back." The detectives consented but the lawyer had not waited for them to answer. He rushed Deborah to the bathroom.

Deborah retched and the tea she had that morning came back up. When she finally felt there was nothing left in her, she washed her face and exited the lavatory to find that the kind lawyer had gotten her a glass of water and a cool cloth.

"Do you feel up to this? We can reschedule

if you like," he said.

"No, I need to get this over with. I can do it." Deborah straightened her spine and walked resolutely back into the library. "I'm sorry, detectives; I'm ready." She picked up the folder and looked at the terrible pictures once again. Her stomach was sick for the little girls in the photos. Some looked as young as four or five years old. How could anyone want to look at children like this? How could anyone put them through it? "These were on Jacob's computer?" she asked.

"Yes. I'm sorry they were."

"I don't recognize any of these children." There had to have been more than a hundred pictures in the folder.

"You're certain?" asked Detective Robinson.

"Yes. I've never seen any of them before."

"Thank you," said the detective. "Do you know a Michelle Henderson?"

"I know of her, but I've never met her."

"How about a Skyler Walker?"

"I don't think so."

"Tamara Martine-Baptiste?"

"I have met her parents at various events."

"Carmen Stovington?"

"I've met her at some Children's Society Events. Um, the Thanksgiving Dinner, and Pet Adoption Day." Those poor children. She grieved for them now much more than herself.

Detective Ruiz handed her four more pictures. These were school pictures of four little blonde-haired girls. "Have you ever seen any of these girls in Mr. Armel's company?"

Deborah could feel the blood drain from her face. These were the girls he was accused of hurting! She scrutinized the pictures. "I never seen Jacob with any of them. I don't think I've ever seen him with any children. He said he had a niece. He bought her gifts. I never met her." She didn't want to believe that the accusations were true, but faced with the disgusting pictures from his computer, she couldn't doubt them any longer. "I never suspected anything. I never saw him interact with a child. He is... I thought he was a nice man, a charming man. I loved him! How could I never see it?" She was crying again despite her resolve not to do so.

"Miss Wade, we may need to speak to you again. And if you think of anything at all, please don't hesitate to call us." Detective Ruiz handed Deborah a business card. "We'll see ourselves out."

"No, that's fine. I'll take you to the door." Mr. Song led the detectives out of the room.

Deborah crumpled back into the chair and closed her eyes. Catherine, Denise, and Simon came into the library. Denise immediately took charge. "Deborah, you are going back to bed. I need you to eat some soup. I'll send one of the girls upstairs with a tray."

"I'm not sick. I don't need to go to bed. I'm not hungry, either." Deborah knew even as she said the words that she didn't sound very convincing.

"You will get sick if you don't eat something. If you don't want to go to bed, that's fine. I want you to rest, read, watch TV, but please just relax." Denise was in full-on doctor mode.

"Okay, I'll eat some soup. But I have to move out of my house. I can't stay there. I need to break it off with Jacob today, as soon as possible. I have to go there and tell him." She was panicked at the thought of confronting him, and it came through in her voice.

Simon spoke up. "Leave it to me to move you out of the cottage. And I think you can ask Jacob Armel to come here for a conversation if you feel he deserves it."

"Deborah, you are moving into Cumberland. I can give you rooms, or I can put you in the guesthouse or the pool house." Catherine Copeland was not asking, she was ordering.

"I don't know what to say," said Deborah.

"All you need to say is whether you prefer rooms in the main house or if you prefer the guesthouse. I think the guesthouse suits you. You'll have privacy; you won't think you're working all the time. Yes. It is decided." She paused. "Well, it is decided if you will acquiesce."

"The guesthouse sounds perfect, but for the next few days, I'll stay here. Is that okay?"

"Oh, my dear! That is perfectly okay." Catherine Copeland hugged Deborah, replaced the blanket, and wiped a tear from her eye.

TRICK ME

Deborah left another message for Jacob. He was not answering his cell. The servants at his house said he had left early that morning with a suitcase and they didn't know where he was. She sighed. She knew he had no intention of explaining things to her or talking to her, and she was not going to have the chance to tell him how she felt. Fleeing was as good as an admission of guilt to her. Slowly but deliberately, she took off the engagement ring she had once thought so beautiful. Now it was an ugly cold piece of metal and a rock. She placed it next to the watch the Armels had given her for Christmas and pulled out her stationery.

Jacob,

You hid your true self from me. Though I can't claim to be happy, I know it is better to have seen your ugly nature revealed before we became man and wife. The horror of that happening while I remained blind will haunt me, but hopefully not forever. I refuse to let you ruin me or my future. You've stolen enough from me. You took the virtue I held so dearly and you didn't even care. I lost my friend because of you. I know that somehow it is your fault. You ruined my reputation, although I couldn't care less about that. You tried to steal my trust. It's been damaged but I will not let it be destroyed. You shattered my heart. You will not take my life, love, or hope. You never loved me. You couldn't have. I realize now that you are as unfeeling as your parents. You're just better at hiding it.

That is the only way you could have done what you did and hidden it so well. But you couldn't hide it forever. Now people know the truth about you. That is good. One day soon, you will face the consequences for the horrible things you have done, for the children you hurt, and the lives you ripped into shreds. You hide now. But you can't hide from yourself.

I hope you learn that I loved you. Even though you didn't love me back, I know you will miss my love. But it will be too late.

Deborah

She put the letter into an envelope and then into a small box with the ring and watch. Robert Song was still at Cumberland talking about strategies with Oliver. Deborah gave the package to him, and he assured her it would go directly to Jacob's hands from his.

She wanted to call Asher. Maybe it would make a difference to him now that she was no longer engaged to Jacob, but she was ashamed that she hadn't seen Jacob as the abhorrent man he was. Besides, she was still hurt by Ash's actions. Ash didn't want her in

Masquerade

his life, so she wouldn't be in his life. There was no point in reaching out just to be hurt by someone else. She needed time to heal, and even though she had lost the people she thought would be her future family, she had not lost the people she thought of as her real family. She still had the Copelands.

Everyone was giving her space, time, and quiet, but she felt as if she needed to be with someone. She called Jackie and poured out her heart about everything. They talked for about two hours and finally ended the conversation when Deborah's phone battery was about to die. She always felt better after talking to her childhood friend. Jackie never judged, and she always seemed to say exactly the right thing.

Deborah was surprised to feel hungry, although it was nearly dinner time. It would be a joy to spend a meal with the family. She went upstairs and freshened up, but didn't change her clothes. Her sweatshirt would have to do. Walking downstairs, she joined Catherine, Oliver, and Sarah in the dining room.

"You didn't have to go to all the effort of coming down here," said Catherine. "We can send a tray up to your room."

"I wanted to be with you all." Deborah took her place at the table, content to realize she did have a place.

"I'm so glad you feel like joining us. It makes me happy to see a little improvement," said Catherine sincerely.

"Deborah," said Oliver, "I'm here for you if

you need me."

"Thank you." Deborah was glad they couldn't talk about the details in front of Sarah, since she had done nothing but talk and think about them the entire day. Dinner was delicious, but she only managed to eat a little bit of it.

Catherine noticed, and ordered a cup of consommé and some cheese and crackers to be brought up to Deborah later. Deborah's broken heart swelled with joy. No one had ever gone out of their way to give her that kind of mother's care before. Her own mother had been too wrapped up in herself to notice Deborah's needs. To have someone meet needs that she never spoke was beyond her hopes, yet it happened at Cumberland on a regular basis.

Sarah chatted away, blissfully unaware of the drama. "Daddy and I went to the park this morning. He let me swing almost as high as the trees." She spoke of her father with adoration and of herself with a child's pride. "He let me watch a movie today, too. I sure like watching TV here more than at home. It's like going to a movie theater. I even had popcorn. Daddy said I could as long as I promised to eat my vegetables. And look, I ate all my broccoli even though there was no cheese sauce on it." Her innocent monologue soothed Deborah's heart, and it looked like the rest of the family felt the same way. There was just something so bright and pure about being a child and seeing all the beauty in the world without the ugliness. Sarah, for her part, was happy to have such an attentive audience.

STARTING OVER

The family was gathered for breakfast. Sarah was dressed in her school uniform, ready for the return to school after the winter break. Oliver was dressed in a suit. He was going into the office for a half day to begin taking back the work responsibilities he had given up after the accident. Life was returning to normal for everyone. Deborah hoped life would improve for her too.

She was moving into the guesthouse that morning, but the move would only take a short time since Simon had hired men to do the bulk of the work. All Deborah needed was for Tom to give her a ride on the golf cart with the bags she had at the main house. She also planned to dive back into her job when she was done. It had been three days, and Deborah felt as if she needed to get to work, to get her mind thinking about other, more hopeful things.

Because two of the girls who Jacob was accused of molesting were part of the Children's Society, Simon had decided that the society would hire legal representation for them and ensure they each had a guardian ad litmus. The children were wards of the state, and the state would have lawyers, but Simon wanted the children to have their own representation and was considering civil suits against Jacob as well. He and Arvin were meeting with Catherine and scheduling a meeting of the board to discuss the options later. Deborah would not attend either meeting for her own sake and the sake of the cases, but there was a great deal of other work she could get done.

After breakfast Deborah called Tom. She and Elsa, one of the maids, gathered her things, and the three of them loaded up the golf cart. After the half-mile ride to the guesthouse, Tom unloaded the bags, and Elsa and Deborah got to work making the guesthouse into Deborah's home. The house was a pretty bungalow covered in creeping vines and flowers. It had a decidedly fairy tale quality to it with its cross gable roof, oversized chimney, and casement windows. It looked as if Princess Buttercup and Westley might step out of it any moment. Deborah loved the whole thing. She could barely wait to sit in the comfortable reading chair by the fireplace, curled up with Jane Austen or Charlotte Bronte.

She had tried to arrange rent with Catherine, but Catherine had said, "It's time you had a raise. Why don't we make the raise the cost of the rent?" She then handed Deborah a prepared contract to that effect, and would not take no for an answer. The lease was good for as long as Deborah chose to live there. It even included a provision for if

Deborah chose not to work for Catherine any longer, but Deborah couldn't fathom ever wanting to leave her job.

Elsa dusted and vacuumed the house while Deborah arranged her things as she wanted them. In an hour they were done, and walked back to the main house together. Deborah felt good for the first time in days; she was excited to get back to work and was already thinking about what paperwork she needed to gather for the accountant so he could prepare the quarterly taxes. She reached her office, sat behind her desk, and was welcomed by her trusty office chair. The computer monitor lit up, and Deborah dove into her work.

Hours passed as she caught up on work that had gone undone. She took a break for lunch and was happy to embrace her newly returned appetite. Her phone rang while she ate a roast beef sandwich; the caller ID revealed the call was from the office of Song and Murdock, Attorneys at Law. "Hello," she said, her stomach tightening a little as she put the sandwich down.

"Is Deborah Wade available?" asked a businesslike feminine voice.

"This is she," answered Deborah. "How can I help you?"

"This is Grace Davison from Song and Murdock. Mr. Song would like you to know that he delivered your package this morning to the promised recipient at his office in Manhattan. Mr. Song received a signed receipt, and there should be no problem."

"Was there any reply?" Deborah wasn't sure what she wanted the answer to be.

"No, there was no reply."

"Thank you." The call ended and Deborah had to consider how she felt. She was relieved the engagement was officially over, yet wondered why Jacob had not said anything or called. Part of her still hoped none of this was true. She wanted him to call and offer her some explanation of what had happened, how the police had it all wrong, and then beg her to forgive him. The longer he didn't call, the more she knew he was guilty. She wondered if he had loved her at all, and she wondered if the times he had been too busy to talk it was because he was destroying a little girl like Jessica or Skyler. Then the doubt began to creep in. Was any part of this her fault? If Deborah hadn't resisted his sexual advances, if his appetite had been filled by someone his own age, would he have stopped going after children? In her head Deborah knew that the choice was his alone and that no one was to blame except him, but she couldn't make those nagging accusations go away.

She threw the remains of her sandwich away and headed back to the office to bury herself in her work. Her heart ached, and she longed to call Ash. He would have calmed her, and he would have told her it wasn't her fault that Jacob had done what he'd done. Even so, she couldn't help feeling like she should have seen signs and been able to stop him. She couldn't call Ash, though, couldn't depend on his counsel now. He would have told her to pray. Ash had let her down, Jacob had let her down. Could she say God had let her down?

She wasn't sure; even though her world was collapsing, at least she wasn't alone. The Copelands had gathered around her. Deborah had left the little house she thought she loved and was given a much better one. She had lost her family and the family she thought she was going to have, only to discover a better family than she could have imagined. She was hurting, she was let down, she was brokenhearted, and she was crushed, but she was not destroyed. There was no reason not to pray, so she bent her head down.

"God, why did this happen? How did I not see the truth? Help those little girls, the ones they know about and the ones they don't." Her voice picked up in intensity. "Make him face punishment. Stop him! Don't let one more child get hurt because of him." Her mind was rambling with a hundred things she wanted to say. "Why did Ash tell me to stay away? Tell him I need him! Tell him I'm sorry for whatever it was I did." Words failed, so she stopped for a minute and breathed. Then she began to think of all that God had done for her. It was as if He were whispering to her heart and calming her spirit. "Thank you for the people who helped me and who love me. Thank you for Denise, Simon, Oliver, and Catherine. Thank you for Mr. Song, Maria, Tom, Irving, Ian, Charlotte, and Elsa. Thank you for my cottage, for my job, for everything. How did I survive all this time, except for you?" She had a million things to thank God for, and kept on thanking Him. She still felt heartsick, but she felt comforted too. Yes, Ash would have told her to pray and she decided she would keep praying every day.

QUESTION

Oliver sat with his head in his hands, not touching the lunch that sat before him. Deborah knew he had another headache. He'd come home from work nearly every day with a headache, and though he didn't complain often, there were times he couldn't hide his pain. "I'm okay," he said when he saw the concern on Deborah's face. "It's stressful trying to keep up. But I know I can do it, and it'll be okay."

"I've got some aspirin if you'd like some." She stood to get him the pills and some water.

"No, thank you. I don't want to take pills." Oliver groaned. "I think I'll get a massage. Do you have the number for the..." He paused, searching for the right word through the distracting pain. "Uh... massage therapist Kelly used?"

"I do, but there are other ones you can use. I won't ask you to take pills you don't want to take, but at least go lie down in a dark room for an hour. Sarah will be home from school at three-fifteen and I know you don't want her to see you this way."

"I'll take the pills after all, thanks, and

then I'll lie down. Can you call a therapist and make an appointment, please? I know it's not your job, but I can barely think."

"Oliver, it's no problem. Go rest. I'll bring you the aspirins and I'll call the masseuse. I'm pretty sure I can get him to come straight away."

Gratitude was plain on Oliver's face as he ascended the stairs. "Thank you, Deborah."

She was worried about him; maybe he was getting back to work too soon, or maybe he needed to only go in a couple of days each week. He had worked full time for the past three weeks and had come home with headaches on half of those days. She quickly did all she had promised she would do. The Copeland name worked wonders with the Belle Cay Spa, and a therapist arrived at the manor an hour after she hung up the phone.

Deborah had returned to work by then, and was engrossed in organizing charitable donations when her phone rang. It was Detective Ruiz, and Deborah was immediately back in the unhappy present. "Hello, this is Deborah. What can I do for you, Detective?"

"Miss Wade, I'm not sure you heard, but Mr. Armel pleaded not guilty to his charges this morning. Detective Robinson and I are solidifying the case against him. We have some questions. I also wanted to let you know that you may be called as a witness."

"I'll do what I can to help, but I doubt I can be of any use. I was clueless."

"I think that as you answer questions you may come up with details which might support other evidence. May I come by this afternoon and talk?"

"Meet me at the Cumberland Manor guesthouse. When are you coming?"

"I'll be there in thirty minutes if that's okay."

The detectives were right on time. Deborah invited them inside and they all gathered in the comfortable living room. They asked her step by step questions about various times she had been in Jacob's home. The interview revealed there was a room in his house she had never been into, a locked door she had seen once and forgotten. The locked door was circumstantial and flimsy evidence, but it bolstered the detectives' confidence in the case. They would add it to a new search warrant. The locked door now frightened Deborah. The interview also brought to mind Jacob's extreme privacy about his laptop. Deborah remembered several times when Jacob closed it abruptly at her entrance and locked it away.

"Once," Deborah said, "we were planning to go to Belleshore for a movie. He had put the laptop in his briefcase just as I entered. The briefcase was right next to him. We needed to check movie times, so I reached toward his bag to get the computer and he shouted at me. It was completely out of character for him. He had never raised his voice before. It scared me. He apologized, but... it stuck with me. I couldn't imagine why he would be upset with me touching the briefcase. I had gone into it several times before. It made no sense at the time. He checked the movie times on his phone, which was across the room on the charger."

"Did you ever find anything unusual in his briefcase on the occasions you opened it?" asked Detective Robinson.

Deborah considered it. "Yes, now that you mention it, he had hair ribbons in the bottom of it, several different ribbons. I barely noticed them, and I never thought to ask him about them." Her stomach dropped. "I should have known; I should have at least wondered! I could have stopped him!"

"No, you couldn't possibly have deduced what he was doing from something like ribbons." Detective Ruiz' words offered little comfort. "Was there anything else?"

"He bought gifts on a few occasions for a child he called his niece even though he said she was the daughter of a friend. I never met her or her parents. I guess now she didn't exist. He was buying gifts for his victims."

The detectives took a list of what toys he had bought and when. Once again Detective Ruiz asked the question, "Is there anything else you can remember?"

"I don't think so. Well, there were a few times I called or went to his house to talk to him and he would cut me off, very abruptly, and tell me he was busy. There were a few times when it was late at night, eleven or twelve o'clock. I have begun to think he may have had the girls with him at those times." She was silent for a few moments. "Is he in jail? Am I allowed to visit him?"

"He posted bail. You are free to talk to him until you receive a court summons. If you do talk to him, we might want to put a wire on you."

Deborah was taken aback by Detective Robinson's statement. "I'll think about it. I don't know if I want to talk him. I'm just so curious. I want answers from him." She put her tea cup down, hopeful that the interview might soon be over.

The detectives stood up, and Anna Ruiz said, "We want them, too. Thank you for your help. If you do decide to talk to him, consider the wire. We could be a layer of protection for you, in case he should decide to threaten you."

Deborah saw them out and sat down in the big armchair. She had a lot to think about, so she put on her coat and went out to the gardens to take a walk and pray. Oliver and Sarah had beaten her to the strolling garden. She could overhear Oliver quizzing his daughter in math while they walked, but when Sarah saw Deborah she took full advantage of the reprieve.

"Miss Deborah!" Sarah skipped over, stopped short of hugging her and instead did a little curtsy. She tried very hard to emulate her regal grandmother.

Deborah hugged the girl. "Well, Miss Sarah, how was your day?"

"It was fine, but I got a C on my math test, so Daddy's helping me study. Instead of using my book, we're counting clouds and trees and branches. He's a genius." She said the last part in a matter of fact tone; she didn't doubt it for a moment.

Oliver smiled. "Yes, I think I might be. Sarah, why don't you go choose a dress to wear to the restaurant tonight? I'll be up in a few minutes."

"Yes, daddy." She skipped off towards the house.

Deborah turned to Oliver, "Are you feeling better?"

"Yes, much, thank you. The masseuse said I was carrying all my stress in my neck and shoulders and that's why I've had a headache. I'll get checked by the doctor, but I think I'm just worrying too much. Work is much harder than it ought to be. My memory problems really show up when I'm trying to juggle details and get things done. I don't want to be a figurehead, and I want my employees' respect. That's hard when I can't remember how to get to my office or when I forget a meeting. Add in this divorce with Kelly and I'm always worrying about something."

Deborah had an idea. "I was going to start going to church this week. Bellshore Community Fellowship meets at eleven in the morning. Why don't you join me? It couldn't hurt. I'm sure it will help both of us." She told him about her new effort to pray, and how she felt peace whenever she did. She had even started to feel that peace when she wasn't actually praying.

"I think I will. That sounds good. It's been a long time since I've gone to church. I used to go all the time. You might even say I was a committed Christian. After the accident, I couldn't go much. Then Kelly started hitting and yelling and I just got angry with God. She wanted to go to keep up appearances, but I was so angry with God that I used the accident as an excuse not to go. After a while it was normal not to go. I think maybe I'm ready to give it a try again."

"You know I was angry with God too. I grew up in church but..." Deborah paused. "Things happened and I blamed God. I'm tired of blaming Him for what evil people do."

"Did you know Simon and Denise go there? I think that's the one, anyway. I know it's not in Belle Cay." Oliver put a reminder in his phone to call Simon.

"I didn't know that. It would be great if they do. If it turns out they don't, maybe we can try their church next."

"Ah, a family affair! We'll invite mother, too. If nothing else she'll enjoy criticizing the outfits." Oliver laughed, and Deborah was glad to see him look happy.

She felt privileged to be included in the family like that. "You know your mother isn't that bad when it comes to talking about people."

Catherine Copeland entered the room and interrupted, "Very true, Deborah. Oliver," she said with a glint of good humor, "I may criticize, but I only critique those who should know better."

BRAND NEW SUN

Belleshore Community Fellowship was a clapboard chapel near the bridge from Belle Cay to Belleshore. Walking in with a group of people instead of alone was a nice feeling. Deborah was pleasantly surprised to see people wearing all kinds of clothes. Some people were dressed in jeans. One man was dressed in overalls and work boots as if he had taken a break from working a farm. There were some who like, the Copelands were dressed more traditionally. The people were welcoming and kind. It seemed all of the two hundred people there introduced themselves. Deborah wasn't sure if she remembered more than two or three names,

    The pastor was a large and gregarious man with salt-and-pepper hair, named Allen Kennedy. His sermon was intriguing and inspiring; he had talked about not worrying and about how God takes care of those who let Him, even the lilies and the birds. He had said people who sought God's kingdom and righteousness didn't have to worry about anything. Deborah thought she might like to talk with him and ask him questions, but wasn't ready yet. It would be nice if she could learn how not to worry. She had so much on her mind and couldn't imagine how letting it all go meant she would have her needs met. It didn't make sense when she thought about it. She wondered if these people were just using religion to ignore their problems.

After the service, the family decided to go to lunch at a Belleshore restaurant that Simon and Denise had recommended, called Green Feast. The eatery was one of Denise's favorites because it offered healthy fare for a variety of diets. It was decorated tastefully in a country farm motif, and Deborah could see why the couple enjoyed it. The friendly waitress came to the table and took everyone's orders. Deborah almost couldn't choose, and in the end ordered mushroom brie soup.

The family talked about impressions of the church service, the people, and the pastor. All had enjoyed it. Denise was thrilled everyone had come. "I've been attending this church for about two years. I like Pastor Kennedy. He's helped me through some difficult times. I accepted Jesus as my Savior last January and was baptized on Valentine's Day."

"Really?" said Deborah. "You are not like the Christians I remember from my childhood." She cut herself off before saying more. She knew some people who said they were Christians but acted like they were better than other people, and thought they could do no wrong while they pointed their fingers at everyone else. Her father's church had stuck by his side throughout his trial and probably even when he was serving his prison time.

Deborah realized she didn't know whether he was still in prison or had been released. She hoped he was still there.

The conversation had continued without her and she came to it to hear Simon talking, "They've supported me through this whole drinking thing. Rich Jefferson is one of the deacons, and he calls me every day to make sure I'm okay. I got a call from him one night just before I was about to take a drink of whiskey."

"Well," said Catherine, "then I am a fan of Rich Jefferson, Allen Kennedy, and this church."

Just then a woman approached the table, tall and slim, with shoulder-length raven-black hair. She would have been quite attractive if not for her the dark circles under her tired eyes, but when she spoke her voice was hot acidic anger. "You!" She pointed at Deborah "You are the floozy who was with that monster who hurt my baby! How could you? Do you know what you did to her? My Michelle has nightmares. She won't talk to people anymore. She used to be a happy little girl, but now she is a frightened silent prisoner!' Her voice grew more shrill with each word. She slapped Deborah across the face. "You deserve to die for what you did to my baby and all those others! There are more, many who won't come forward and can't come forward!"

The restaurant manager finally appeared. "Mrs. Henderson, please, come this way." He gently took the woman by the arm and led her to the far side of the restaurant, saying something quietly to a waitress as he passed.

Deborah sat stunned. Her face stung. She tried to gather herself. "I'm sorry... I am so sorry." She began crying and wanted to reach out to the woman but there was nothing she could say that would make it better.

The waitress came to the table. "I'm sorry but your presence is disturbing some of our guests. While we understand that it is not your fault, and you were the victim of an uncalled-for attack, we hope you will understand what Mrs. Henderson is going through and forgive her. Meanwhile, I need to ask you to leave. You are welcome to return at another time. Please consider this meal a gift from the restaurant, and we would also like to extend a complimentary dinner when you choose to come back."

"What meal? We've only ordered; we haven't received more than waters." Simon was clearly angry. "We'll leave. I doubt we'll return."

"I'm sorry," said Deborah, turning to Mrs. Copeland. "Should I pay for their lunch?"

"No, dear, she wouldn't want that. This really has nothing to do with you. She needed to blame someone, and you happened to be available." She turned to the apologetic waitress. "We understand. This is a lovely restaurant and I am sure we will return." She wrapped her hand around Deborah's and walked her out to the car.

In the car Deborah was no longer crying, but she wondered anew if she were to blame somehow. If he could have satisfied his lust with her, would he have turned to the little girls? How many girls had Jacob done this to? How many girls had her father and her uncle hurt? Oliver and Catherine offered her kind words. They reminded her it wasn't her fault and that Jacob was depraved. Regardless how much sex he got from women, they told her, he still would have attacked the children.

She knew it was true, but Mrs. Henderson's slap felt no less deserved. "Thank you" was all she managed to say for about ten minutes as she considered everything. At last she said, "Mrs. Henderson was right about Jacob Armel. He is a monster. But she was wrong about me. None of this is my fault. I don't know how I ever thought I loved him, or if I did at all. I need to talk to him. I need to settle this for myself." She hated him, and it reminded her of the hate she felt for her father and her uncle. That hate had been forcibly buried; she had made herself into a person who hated no one, a kind person who would never dream of hurting someone else. Suddenly, though, she knew that persona was a lie. She hated at least five men. She had dreamed a hundred dreams of hurting her uncle and a hundred more of hurting her father. She had envisioned their ruin, had watched her father go to prison and had hoped he would be beaten as the child molester he was. Fervently, she hoped the same fate awaited her ex-fiancée, but at the same time she didn't want all this hate inside her. It had surprised her to find all the bitterness still lurking under the surface; she had thought it was gone, but it had only been buried. Jacob had resuscitated it.

Deborah dialed Jacob's number and was not surprised that it went to voicemail. "Hello. I want to see you. I want to talk. You owe me that. Call me back or text me, I don't care. Just let me know when I can meet you at your office."

"Whenever that is," said Catherine, "you can use the jet and we'll take the day, maybe even a few days, in New York. Some part of the trip can be pleasurable."

Deborah gratefully accepted the offer.

Masquerade

YOU'RE SO VAIN

Grayson International had begun more than a century earlier by supplying medications to the American and Canadian armies, but had grown to be a worldwide pharmacological researcher, manufacturer, and distributor. Jacob Armel was the CEO. Deborah stood outside his Manhattan offices, steeling herself to see him again. He had sent a text with nothing more than a day and time. She had shown up with no idea how this was going to go or if she was ready, but she needed to do it.

She walked into his outer office and was greeted by a professionally pleasant man. "How may I help you?"

"I'm Deborah Wade, I have an appointment with Mr. Armel for ten o'clock." She straightened her skirt so that it met her knees.

The assistant picked up the phone, and spoke quietly. "Please have a seat," he said to Deborah. "He will be with you shortly." He then returned to whatever work he was doing and ignored her. Ten long minutes later the phone buzzed. The assistant spoke quietly again, then looked up from his work to

Deborah. "You may go in now." He got up and opened the office door.

Deborah entered the spacious modern gray and black office. Jacob sat behind a large shining black desk. He stood and showed her the small black leather chair she could sit in. "Have a seat." He said it as if she were a client or employee, not his ex-fiancée. He didn't even offer his hand to her. 'What can I do for you?"

"What can you do for me?" Deborah was incredulous. "I'm not here on business! I want answers!"

"What could my answers possibly do for you, Deborah?"

"Did you love me?" She wanted to know but doubted he would answer truthfully.

"I do love you." For all the feeling in his voice, he might as well have said, "I'll have the coffee." He stood up and walked to the front of his desk, leaning back on it. The move reminded Deborah of something people did in movies. "I was giving you space. I didn't want to involve you in the scandal." His affect was nearly emotionless. At that moment he truly sounded like his parents.

Deborah didn't believe him, and she wondered if he even believed himself. "Did you do those things?"

Jacob sighed. "No. Of course not. How dare you question me? Did you love me?"

She ignored the question. "There is so much compelling evidence against you. It seems pretty certain to me that you did the things they say you did. But I'd like to believe you. How do you explain it?"

He crossed his legs and arms. "I didn't do anything. I was kind to those little girls. I let them swim in my pool and play with toys in my home. I was kind. Someone misconstrued my kindness." There was no emotion in the words he recited.

"I want to believe you." Deborah wanted so badly to believe that everything was just a big misunderstanding. Now more than ever, though, she knew he was guilty. The man who stood before her was not the man he had pretended to be for so long. The gregarious and charming veneer was gone; in his place there stood an actor or an animatronic man.

"My love," said Jacob as he continued his performance, "I'm glad you chose Valentine's Day to visit me. You can believe me, I promise." He walked to a safe behind his desk and brought out two boxes. One was a black velvet ring box, the other was also black velvet but flatter and larger. "I want to give you back your engagement ring. Maybe you fell for the deception. People are lying to you. But I intend to make you my wife." He opened the ring box, took out the ring, and waited in a gesture of asking for her hand. "And I won't ask you to sign the pre-nuptial agreement. That should prove my sincerity."

"What? You are kidding. Right?" Deborah did not give him her hand. "You have not seen me since New Year's Eve, haven't answered a call or a text or called me at all. I am not sure what you think love is, but it isn't this. I just told you I think you're a child molester! Have you heard a single word I've said? Have you ever heard a word I've said?"

He was undeterred and unruffled. "Okay. We might not be ready to jump right back in where we left off. As time goes by I think you'll begin to understand that I was protecting you. I was giving you space and keeping you from the gossip. I'll hold onto this until you're ready." He put the ring back in the box and placed it in his jacket pocket, then opened the next one and held the open box toward her. Inside was a slender gold chain, and on the end was a gold heart with diamonds forming the letter D in the corner. "Wear this and be reminded that you are my heart." His words were meaningless and hollow; they sounded like the GPS on Deborah's phone giving voice directions.

"Jacob, we are no longer in a relationship. I thought I loved you. I don't know who I loved but it wasn't you; it was some character you portrayed. I will not marry you and I will not be seeing you anymore." She wanted answers but doubted he could or would give them to her. "Why were all those photos of children on your computer?"

He sighed and his demeanor became even flatter than it already was. "Someone probably planted them there. I'm worth more money than many people could ever hope to be. If someone were to oust me from my position and standing, they could gain some of that for themselves. Do you understand that I'm facing prison? I need a wife by my side. I need to show the jury I'm not the man the prosecutors are painting me to be."

Deborah breathed harder as she tried to understand him. Did he even think anyone could believe what he was saying? "That plot wouldn't even make sense in a movie. And really? You want me to marry you so the jury will think you're a nice guy? Did you pursue me because you thought you could fool me?"

"I pursued you because you are beautiful. You are equal to me in every way that I require, and complement me in every way that I need. I love you."

"Stop throwing that word around as if it means something to you!" At least one of them would show some emotion in this meeting.

"Deborah, I do love you. I'm sorry you feel unworthy of that love. You are beautiful, and many men have and will love you. Look at that Asher of yours." Jacob shook his head in pity for the many men who would not have his bride. "Most love you from afar, but I was courageous enough to love you intimately."

Deborah was stunned to hear Jacob say Ash loved her. She didn't have time to mull over whether it could be true or not. "You do not know what love is, Mr. Armel. You don't know much more about me than what I look like. There is no intimacy in that kind of love. That is desire and lust, not love. Any act within that was not love either. You used me; you conquered me. But I have taken myself back. I'm free." She stood up, turned around and walked to the door. "Goodbye." She felt she had been a bit overdramatic, but maybe high drama was the only thing Jacob could understand.

She left his offices and the gleaming building that contained them, walking briskly to the doorman who called her waiting car for her. Quickly she got in, thanking the doorman and the driver. She had expected to cry, but her eyes were dry, and her broken heart felt better and stronger. It was a happy thing not to be stuck with Jacob's façade forever. She was ready to move forward.

ME TIME

Catherine Copeland and Deborah sat side by side in the ritzy spa, in comfortable thick chairs, having pedicures. Both women were enjoying a full day of spa treatments including facials, manicures, pedicures, wraps, steam baths, salt rooms, and massages. Deborah had never indulged in such a luxury before, but the relaxation and quiet suited her. Soft new age music played on hidden speakers in the dimly lit room.

"Ash is in the city," said Deborah. She missed her old friend. Even though she was still hurt by his sudden abandonment of her, she could really use his compassion right now.

"Is he?" responded Catherine. "Maybe you'll spot him somewhere before we go back to Cumberland."

Deborah laughed. "New York City is a little bit bigger than Belle Cay, Connecticut. I don't think there is much chance of me accidentally bumping into him. Besides, I'm still processing the breakup with Jacob. I can't handle arguing with Ash." Part of her longed to "spot" Ash, but part of her dreaded the idea.

"Do you think what Mr. Armel said is

true? Do you think Ash is in love with you?"

"If he loved me, why would he ask me to give him distance? Why wouldn't he fight for me? Where is he now if he loves me?"

Catherine thought for a moment and said, "True love longs for the object of his love to be happy. Does he know what you're going through? This Armel case is taking up almost your whole world right now, but most people don't know about it. I have a feeling if that young man knew you needed him, he'd be by your side."

"You think he loved me?" Deborah was more than perplexed; she was downright bewildered that she could have missed something everyone else seemed to find obvious.

"Yes. I knew it from the moment I met him. I knew you loved him too from the first time you spoke about him." Catherine had no malice or teasing in her voice.

"I love him? No... I was in love with Jacob."

"You were in love with who you thought Jacob was. You were in love with the idea of being in love with him, but in truth, you were falling in love with Asher Levine."

A young woman entered the room and asked Catherine and Deborah to follow her. She led each of them to separate rooms, where Catherine would have her massage and Deborah would have her facial.

As Deborah lay on the table with eyes closed and the esthetician worked a cream onto her skin, she had to contemplate the idea that she loved Ash. She knew that around Ash she had always been happy and comfortable. No matter what she was wearing or how little effort she had put into her appearance, he was pleased to see her. She could smile, laugh, cry, act silly, or speak about life's mysteries with Ash. If she were honest with herself, she had to admit that Jacob was not someone she could act silly with or talk with about the deep questions. Maybe she had come to love Ash more deeply than a friend, but then again he had never acted on any feelings he might have had. Jacob had outright wooed her, while Ash had certainly seemed content to be just her friend. Even so, where was he now, and why had he discarded her? Whatever he might once have been, whatever could once have happened, it was all for naught now. She was angry, hurt, devastated. It would be easy enough to find Ash; she could call him, or find out where the record label offices were, or see if Epsilon were doing a show. She just wasn't ready for another confrontation, though; she needed to recover from the last one. At last the train of thoughts was forcibly stopped, and Deborah began praying while she relaxed into her spa day.

That evening the women emerged from the St. Regis spa looking and feeling beautiful. Both were perfectly coiffed and wore new outfits, Catherine's a royal blue empire waist dress adorned with delicate crystals and Deborah's an off-the-shoulder black cocktail dress. To embellish the outfit she had a piece of art jewelry made of metallic leaves in various colors of gold, copper, pinks, and greens forming a necklace. Her new shoes were a pink gold color that matched her new purse perfectly. They stepped into the waiting Bentley and were whisked off to dinner and then to a Broadway show.

The time in New York had been a whirlwind of shopping, sightseeing excursions, and evenings on the town, all carefully planned by Catherine Copeland to lighten Deborah's heavy heart. All that "retail therapy" was doing its job. Deborah would be happy to get back home again, but she was also sad to see the week come to an end.

Catherine must have read her mind, "We still have tonight and tomorrow morning to enjoy. Stay in the moment and let tomorrow come when it is time."

Deborah chose to do just that.

BEAUTIFUL GOODBYE

Deborah put her new clothes away and enjoyed the trip all over again in her mind as she carefully hung each new outfit. There would be no need to buy clothes for a very long time, but since it was so much fun she probably would anyway. The thought made her laugh; it was so out of character for her normal careful and responsible self. She had spent a few thousand dollars of her savings account that weekend, but she didn't regret it, nor was she worried. Her job paid well and her expenses were minimal. She decided she could handle being carefree every now and then. At the same time that she put new clothes in her closet, though, she took some old ones out and put them in a box of donations for Belleshore Community Fellowship clothing drive.

She decided to join the Copelands for dinner that night, as she was tired from the trip and didn't have anything fresh in the fridge to cook for dinner. On the walk over to the house, she met a very happy Oliver.

"Guess what Mr. Song just delivered?" he asked, holding a thick manila envelope. "These are the divorce papers! I've signed them and they are ready to be delivered to Kelly."

"Will she sign?" Deborah asked.

"I hope so. I'm being more than generous, considering I don't have to be. I think she will sign if she knows what's best. I could still have her arrested. I could even enforce the pre-nup; Mother wants me to, but whatever Kelly is and whatever she's done, she is Sarah's mother. I don't want Sarah to grow up hating either of us, and I want this to be as easy as possible for her. The divorce alone will cause enough trauma without adding more."

"Oliver," Deborah said hugging him, "I don't know if any man in this world is quite the amazing man you are."

He blushed, "Thanks. I love Sarah. Her happiness, safety, and future are more important than my bitterness or vengeance against Kelly."

The days that followed had their share of up and downs. Numerous upcoming plans for the spring kept Deborah busy every moment she was at work. The gala season was approaching. The various wealthy Belle Cay residents would each attend most of them, and many would throw one of their own. Deborah was getting ahead of the game by organizing what she could. As long as she was busy, she didn't think too much about what might have been with Ash. She still occasionally thought about Jacob, but only when something popped up in the news. She no longer hurt for herself, but the pain for the children would never go away. It was proving impossible to reconcile the man she had loved with the monster who had destroyed those children. He was two different people to her.

Although she tried not to admit it, the entire situation had brought her own childhood traumas back. She had been having nightmares since January and had found herself not trusting men. Yet somehow she was dealing with it. There was a huge difference between the way she handled it as a child and the way she handled it as an adult. As a child she had withdrawn into herself. She had run off to be alone as a teenager. As an adult, though, she wrapped herself into the family that had wrapped itself around her. She didn't pull away and stop talking; she talked about things and embraced people. There was also this new church and this new search for God.

Whatever Kelly might have been thinking, whatever fury might have been coursing through her veins, she seemed to know better than to fight the divorce. She signed the papers after holding on to them for a week. Deborah felt that was just to torture Oliver, but Kelly had no idea how confident Oliver was becoming when he was no longer under her thumb. The woman didn't stay in Belle Cay for long after the papers were signed. She left to some unnamed place, only saying a quick goodbye to the child she had birthed and the man she claimed to have once loved.

Time was moving on for everyone. Some

parts were painful, some were joyful, and all worked together to fill days and hearts with life and living.

Masquerade

YOU'LL NEVER WALK ALONE

The weather was perfect for a hike in the woods, and Deborah decided to take advantage of the mild day. Her backpack was filled with the necessities: water, granola, a turkey wrap, a thermos of broth, and most importantly chocolate. She headed down a trail she had not yet tried, breathed in the beautiful country air and breathing out her troubles. The trees loomed high overhead and birdsong filled the maple-scented air while Deborah blissfully walked along the trail. As always, walking sparked contemplation, but unlike in prior years, the contemplation became prayer.

"God, I'm done with the past. I'm ready to enjoy the here and now. I'm ready to look forward to the future. How do I do that? I'm done with Jacob. I'm really thankful that he's out of my life. I'm done thinking of Ash. If he loved me like everyone says he does, he'd be here with me. He would have fought for me. He would have protected me."

You never needed Ash to protect you. You've had me.

Deborah heard the words clearly. They

were thoughts without words, and words without thoughts, almost like thought, but more like an impression that she couldn't explain. She knew it wasn't her voice. Was it God? "Have you protected me? Where were you when my uncle did those things to me? Where were you when my mother treated me like I was an annoyance instead of a daughter? Where were you when my dad hurt Daisy?"

I was with you, my beloved baby girl. People do evil things. I do not.

"You were? I know it wasn't you that hurt me; it was them. It just hurts. So much hurts. How do I go on?"

You go with me. Take my hand. Stop holding back. Find out who I am.

"I don't know how to find you. Do I talk to the pastor at the church? Do I read the Bible? I don't have one. I can pick one up. I don't know if I can understand everything in there. Anyway, is that gonna give me a future? You know I want to find a husband and start a family someday. What if I can never trust a man enough to love him or let him love me? I'm afraid even to ask you to send me a man. I'm not ready to lose myself to a man, but oh, I really want to...one day."

This time there was no answer, but strangely, Deborah didn't feel like she needed one.

The woods were so picturesque. Deborah stood still and looked at the beauty that surrounded her, then drank some water and checked her watch, surprised to find she had been walking for nearly an hour. She pulled out her granola and snacked as she walked a little farther along the footpath, eventually coming to a fork in the trail. After half a moment's thought, she went to the right.

"God, this is such an amazingly exquisite world. Thanks for making it. I think I love Ash. I know I do. I miss him. Do I call him? Do I try to get him back? Do I just leave him in the past and hope to love someone else one day?"

A sparrow flew in front of her and ate seeds off the path. She remembered the sermon from her first Sunday at the church in Belleshore. The pastor had read a passage from the Bible. Jesus had said birds didn't worry, but God took care of them, and that all a person had to do was seek God and He would take care of everything else. Deborah wanted to laugh; she wanted to sing out loud. God had spoken again, this time through a tiny bird in the forest. "Okay, I'll try it your way, I won't worry about some future husband. I'll take some time and get to know you."

The breeze kissed her nose. She breathed in the wonderful air and breathed out all her stresses and cares. The path offered her another choice, and she went to the right.

The next day Deborah went to a bookstore and looked through the array of Bibles and journals and gear to go with them. She had called the pastor and asked what kind of Bible she should buy, and he had suggested an English Standard Version, or, if she were concerned about difficulty understanding it, to get The Message. She decided to get both, along with a leather journal, a pack of highlighters, bookmarks, and a very nice pen. She was excited about this new venture and was diving into it with all of her Deborahesque enthusiasm.

After checking out, she took her purchases to the in-store coffee shop, broke open the Bibles, and turned to the book of John, where Pastor Kennedy had suggested she begin. After reading the first chapter in The Message and then in the other Bible, she read it a couple of verses at a time, comparing versions often.

Pastor Kennedy had told her it was important not to stress over anything she didn't understand, and that he would be happy to answer any questions. The whole situation felt a little awkward to Deborah; she had gone to church for most of her childhood, yet she had never read the Bible on her own. She had thought she loved God, but wondered now if she had really loved the idea of God, the idea of the perfect families she thought she saw in church week after week, and the idea of security she imagined the church offered her. It was beginning to dawn on her that she had professed to love God, but she didn't really know Him.

LETTING GO

The Belle Cay Star front page reported that Jacob's trial had started and that he had pleaded not guilty to the long list of charges. Deborah had not been called as a witness, although she knew the defense was considering it. They changed their minds after apparently deciding that she would be hostile and not likely to give a good character reference to her ex-fiancée. That was fine with Deborah; she was very grateful not to have to take the stand for either side.

She read the article begrudgingly, almost as if she were compelled to do so. The article mentioned the girls but withheld their identities. Deborah was certain there was not a person in Belle Cay who didn't know the name of each of the four victims in the case, but she hoped that more than their identities would be protected as the case went forward. She was grateful that they were each in counseling. Civil suits were already being pursed on behalf of all of them.

The paper lay open on the table, her toast and tea growing cold as she remembered the nightmare of her father's case. She had been the prosecution's star witness. Her ability to testify had saved little Daisy from the trauma of being called to the stand. It had been awful to point her finger at the man who had raised her, had been horrendous to be called a spiteful liar and to have him look at her with loathing the entire time. She remembered her mother's testimony, denying everything Deborah had said and then renouncing her as her own daughter.

Daisy had not had to suffer the trial. She had not had to face the beast who had shattered her life and relive every gruesome detail. Skyler, Michelle, Carmen and Tamara would likely have to. Even if they did it via a camera from another location and didn't have to look at Jacob, they would still have to recall the horror of what he had done.

The phone rang; the caller ID told her it was Candice Lowery. Deborah knew she didn't want to talk to the reporter, nor did she have anything of value to add to any legitimate news report. She contemplated answering it, but let it go to voicemail. The reporter had left three that day and ten over the last three days. The sudden sound had brought Deborah out of her reverie, so she finished her breakfast and got ready for work.

The work day was going well. Deborah and Catherine had laid the foundations for a wonderful spring flower exhibition. Deborah had checked with Arvin and happily discovered he needed no help from her for the Children's Society work. She helped Catherine and Charlotte go through Catherine's closet to collect clothes for the church's clothing drive. Finally she double-checked and approved Ian's household budget. There was nothing more to do by three, so Deborah decided to see if she could find an unread and interesting title in the library.

Oliver had been adjusting to his work days as well. He had fewer headaches now that he had established routines to improve his memory, and had also hired an excellent administrative assistant to support him. He came in from work with Sarah by his side, clearly enjoying the mundane duty of picking her up from school each day. The girl was feeling the loss of her mother, but Oliver was doing his best to lessen that loss.

Sarah was involved in telling her father some convoluted tale of classroom drama. Deborah thought she would have had a hard time feigning interest, but Oliver looked as if he hung on every word. Sarah always did her homework in the library at her late grandfather's huge desk. She continued talking as she and her father entered the room, but when she saw Deborah she dropped the subject of William Heath's bad behavior immediately and greeted her with a hug.

"Miss Deborah," she exclaimed, "Easter is coming and Daddy said he's going to buy me a new dress. I get to pick it out. Will you come shopping with us?

Deborah was honored. She looked at Oliver, who gave his silent consent. "I would love to. When shall we go?"

Oliver spoke up. "Tomorrow will be a good day for us to go. We can pick out a dress, shoes, hat, everything, and get lunch."

"I'll put it on my calendar right away," said Deborah, as she made a show of pulling out her smartphone and adding the date to her schedule. Sarah seemed to crave Deborah's company since her mother had left her. "Do you have homework?" Deborah asked, knowing Fridays usually meant a lighter than normal load. "I was just about to have some afternoon tea."

"I have a math page to do. I'll be done with it lickety split."

"Then, Sarah my dear, I will meet you in the sitting room. Will you join us, Oliver?" Deborah turned to Sarah's father.

"Yes, of course," he said.

Deborah left to arrange a nice afternoon tea for Sarah, complete with finger sandwiches, little cakes, and fine china.

Shopping with Sarah and Oliver was more fun than Deborah had expected. Oliver clearly preferred a woman to help pick out the appropriate dress for Sarah. He wasn't comfortable trying to decide if her dress was fashionable enough to please her and childish enough to please him. There were few quiet moments, as Sarah was able to talk nearly non-stop. By the time they had picked out a sage green dress with a crinoline slip under the skirt, Deborah knew more about William Heath and the rest of Sarah's classmates than she thought possible.

Masquerade

They walked from the lovely little dress shop to a boutique that specialized in hats and scarves in search of just the right hat to match the Easter outfit. At the hat shop, Sarah unexpectedly grew quiet. Her sad eyes looked at a pair of hats, one large and one small, made to fit a mother and daughter. "Mommy hasn't even sent me a card. We liked dressing up the same for Easter and for parties. Daddy always said we were like beautiful twin princesses."

Deborah had no idea what to say. She put her arms around the girl, who suddenly appeared not just small but tiny and fragile.

"Why don't we write her a letter when we get home tonight?" suggested Oliver. He looked as if his daughter's pain was his own.

"Where will we send it?" Sarah was cautiously hopeful.

Oliver hugged his daughter. "I will send it to Grammy and Poppy, and I am sure they will get it to her. You can write them a letter as well. You haven't written them since your Christmas thank-you cards."

Sarah brightened up and leaped into the job of searching for just the right hat.

Donna Campbell

AMAZING GRACE

The church was filled to the rafters for the Easter service. People Deborah saw week after week and people she had never met before crowded every pew, chair, and space. Almost every one of them was dressed as if they were going to the biggest gala of the year. Little girls felt like princesses. Little boys fidgeted in suits they dreamed of taking off. Men and women walked into the church like movie stars on the red carpet.

As the time of the service drew closer, the kids all went off to children's church to enjoy their special lesson and crafts. Deborah was ready to hear the familiar story of the cross and resurrection. Yet the message that day was not like any Easter message she had heard before. Instead, it was about forgiveness. Deborah listened to the pastor talk about the importance of forgiving people. He offered verse after verse and several stories about the power of forgiveness, then quoted a Bible verse that said people were supposed to forgive seventy times seven times. "Consider what you have been forgiven for," he implored the listening crowd. "We are supposed to forgive as many times as we are hurt."

Deborah was starting to get indignant. *Well, Jesus didn't have to forgive a sexual criminal*, she thought. *He didn't have to forgive a friend who betrayed Him. Of course He thinks forgiving is so easy. What have I ever done to need forgiving, anyway?*

The pastor then moved on to Jesus' crucifixion. Deborah listened intently to the story she had heard a hundred times, wondering if God were going to show her something new this time. Allen Kennedy described Judas as one of Jesus' closest friends, and described his betrayal, then talked about Peter a man who really could call himself one of Jesus' best friends, and how even Peter denied him. Jesus had forgiven him. It was as if God were answering her questions through Pastor Kennedy.

Next the pastor described the horror of a crucifixion and what Jesus went through even though he had done nothing wrong to deserve death. Then he said, "Jesus is Emmanuel. He is God with us. He was not born a sinner and He never sinned. I am about to tell you a story that some of you know and some of you don't. When I was in college, I raped a woman. She was drunk, so I took advantage of her condition and had my way with her. I was the lowest of the low. I served much-deserved time in prison for that crime, but that didn't forgive what I had done. In prison, I came to know Jesus. I accepted Him as my savior. Jesus forgave me, a sex offender, and He made me new. Jesus died on the cross for me. He died on the cross for you. Maybe you've never done something as repulsive as what I did. Maybe you've done worse. But you have done things. You've lied, you've had unkind thoughts, you've felt entitled to justice, and you've done countless other things. You may not consider these to be as bad as what I did, but God considers them all to be sins. You haven't done these things just once, either, but hundreds of times, thousands. You have just as much to be forgiven for as I do."

Deborah tried to listen, but her mind was turning itself in circles as the pastor talked about the reason for the celebration, the Resurrection. He talked about the Resurrection giving each person a new life, allowing them to live eternally with Jesus both in the future and now. The words seemed like they were being uttered from a great distance, as Deborah was still reeling from the deathblow that the pastor's words had given to her pride. Tears fell from her eyes as she understood that Jesus had died and rose from the dead for her. He had died to forgive her sins. She understood the weight of forgiveness and unforgiveness only too well. Jesus forgave her, even though He suffered.

Before she knew it the congregation was standing and singing. She jumped up and headed down the aisle as quickly as possible. She didn't care how she looked to the people around her. She went to the pastor, who was waiting in front of the stage, and before he could utter a word she said, "I want Jesus to be my Savior! I'm so sorry; I have done so much wrong and He forgave me. I want to give him my whole life." Her words tumbled out and she doubted they made much sense.

Allen Kennedy gripped her hands and laughed kindly. "My dear, you just did! Welcome to the family." He hugged her and asked her to wait in the front pew while he spoke to and prayed with the others who had come up. Rich Jefferson's wife, Margaret, was there, and she talked with Deborah and asked her questions to make sure she understood what she had just done. Deborah knew she did. Everything she had learned over the years was suddenly real and true. Margaret filled out a paper and asked Deborah if she would like to be baptized.

"Oh, yes! I do. I want to do whatever Jesus wants me to do." Deborah was prepared to do it right then and there, but Margaret told her it would be the following week.

Allen called Deborah up to join him at the front of the church, and introduced her to everyone. The entire congregation stood and applauded. Many people soon surrounded her with hugs and congratulations and prayers.

Donna Campbell

THE HEART OF THE MATTER

Deborah lounged in the big comfortable chair that had become her reading chair. She had done a great deal of praying about forgiving her parents and the many others she needed to forgive. It was not an easy thing to do. "How do I do it, Lord?"

Make peace where you can.

"Okay, make peace. How do I make peace?" Pulling out her lap desk and her stationery, she decided it was time to write her parents a letter. She didn't include any accusations; she let all the blame go, and she simply wrote about her life in Belle Cay. She mentioned Jacob, but only to say they were no longer engaged. It wasn't much, but it was something. She hoped it wouldn't fall on deaf ears.

Could she forgive Jacob? That would be the real test, since she had no desire to restore any relationship with him. She was going to have to talk to Denise about how she could forgive him. She dialed the phone, eager to get it done.

Denise answered on the first ring. "Deborah! How are you?"

"I'm really well, Denise. Thanks. I have to ask you some serious questions, spiritual questions."

"Okay. Let's meet at Cheryle's Coffee Café. Do you know where that is, over on Third Street behind Main?"

"Yes, I can be there in thirty minutes." Deborah could hardly contain her eagerness

"Better make it forty. See you there." Denise ended the call.

Deborah arrived at the coffee shop and found a set of armchairs in a quiet corner. Moments later Denise arrived, wearing her scrubs and hospital ID. "You're working?" Deborah asked in surprise. "You didn't have to meet with me now."

"I am on my dinner break, and if I'm needed I can be paged. You're important to me and I'm honored that you turned to me." Denise made herself comfortable.

The waitress approached, and Denise ordered her typically healthy meal, a sparkling water and a tomato and feta salad.

Deborah ordered a tea and a chocolate cupcake, then wasted no time in getting down to business. "I want to forgive people, but I'm not sure how to forgive people who aren't in my life anymore or people who I don't want in my life. People like my uncle." Deborah paused and looked down for a moment. "And Jacob."

"Forgiveness isn't something you do for those people, Deborah. It's something you do for you, something between you and God. It is about letting go of the blame, letting God be the judge and the giver of justice." Denise took her food from the waitress. "I had to forgive someone who had died. Every day I said it out loud to myself and to God. When I would get angry about what she had done to me, I would purposely let it go. I would choose to remind myself that God was handling it."

Deborah considered her words and took a long sip of the steaming liquid in its dainty cup. "So I don't have to call Jacob, make amends, or anything like that?"

Denise laughed, "This is life with Jesus, not Alcoholics Anonymous. No, you don't have to be friends with him. You can pray for him, pray that God will have His way with him. You can also pray for Jacob's salvation."

"Pray for his salvation? I want him to suffer!" She was holding her cupcake and nearly squeezed it into crumbs at the idea of wanting something good for him.

Denise smiled gently. "Listen, God loves him, even though he did those awful things. God wants him to be saved, so as you learn to love him the way Jesus loves him, you'll want him to be saved too. Start now; pray for it now. He'll either accept Jesus and let Jesus pay for his sins, or he won't and God will have His vengeance. Understand this, Deborah; listen with your ears and with your heart. You're not excusing the monstrous things he did. You're choosing not to let your desire for punishment destroy you."

They talked about some other things before Denise had to head back to the hospital, but Deborah's mind was still stuck on those words. As long as she'd thought forgiving Jacob and her family meant she had to pretend nothing had ever happened, it had been easy to convince herself it wasn't possible. If Denise was right, though, and if forgiveness was something she had to do for her own benefit, then it wouldn't be so easy to make excuses. Sooner or later she would have to dig in and do it.

Perhaps it could be later.

Donna Campbell

TURN TURN TURN

Deborah was at the Belleshore Mall enjoying a rainy day off work when she saw Epsilon's newest CD. Curiosity compelled her to pick it up. As angry as she had been with Ash, she was trying to find the best way to forgive him. More and more, she still had to admit she loved him, regardless of what he felt for her.

She put the CD into the player as soon as she got in the car. The songs were instantly likable; they had hard driving beats and passionate music, with the Epsilon signature melodic interludes between the heavy rock singing. Deborah drove slowly along the scenic route so she had more time to listen to the album. The fifth song struck her; there was something about the tune which seemed familiar to Deborah. She knew she had never heard it, but it spoke to her. The chorus of the song, sung in a mournful tone between the screaming verses, said,

All I have are memories of you.
There are days I long for more,
But they are far and very few.

Masquerade

My life is better off with just memories of you
Anyway, that's the lie I tell myself
That's the lie I need to believe.

Was this song about her? She checked the song title: *Too Far the Distance*. That didn't mean it was about her, but she really felt like it was. She picked up her phone and began to dial Ash, then put it down again. What exactly would she say when she finally got him on the phone? She put the song on again for another listen before moving on to the rest of the album.

On arriving home she found a letter in the mail. The envelope had her mother's familiar handwriting. She held it for a few minutes, turning it over in her hands, savoring the connection to the family she had lost. She was nervous to read it, so she breathed a prayer, sat down in her reading chair, and opened the letter.

Deborah,

I don't know why you think you can send a letter to me as if I care about anything that is happening in your perfect life. I read it only because I hoped you might finally apologize for destroying your father. There was not an iota of regret, not a single word asking for forgiveness. I didn't expect one, and even if you had come here begging on your knees, I could never forgive you. How dare you assume you can be my daughter ever again?

Do you even know what your lies and accusations did? Your father, the man who raised you, protected you, and cared for you, went to prison. He was beaten by other inmates so often that he became a shell of who he was. Three years into his sentence, he was beaten so badly that he died from his injuries. They broke 20 bones in his body, ruptured his spleen, punctured his lungs, and left him to bleed to death. That is on you.

Never, never contact me again. I do not want to hear about your fancy life in your fancy mansion with your fancy friends. I have to work two jobs to pay the bills. I'm a pariah. It is all your fault.
Eileen Wade

Deborah sat stunned and broken. Her father was dead. Her father had suffered and died. He had suffered far worse than she could have imagined. She cried for him; she had lost him years ago and had grieved him years ago, but hadn't known he was killed. The prison sentence may as well have been death.

She pulled out her phone and dialed the phone number of her childhood home.

"Hello," said an unfamiliar voice.

"Um..." Deborah sniffed back her tears. "Is Eileen there?"

"There's no one here by that name. You've got a wrong number, hun." The line went dead.

She held the phone for a few minutes, then pulled out her stationery again. She wrote, "Mom, I'm sorry." She could think of no more to write.

Deborah's mind turned to Jacob. He was going to go to prison, as he deserved, but would he also suffer like her dad had suffered. She'd heard the rumors about what happened to child molesters in prison. She had once wanted him to suffer horribly, but now, although she wanted him to face the consequences of his actions, she didn't want him beaten, maimed, or killed.

The rain had let up and Deborah decided she needed to commune with God in her favorite way. She needed to pray and walk.

Ten minutes later she was on an easy trail at the edge of a nearby wood. Prayers spilled out of her about everything: Asher, Jacob, her parents, her future and theirs. She had left in a hurry without changing into boots, and the muddy ground was ruining her tennis shoes. They became slicker with every step, but she didn't care. She was talking to God, and He was giving her peace even through her tears. She mourned her father. Even though she knew it wasn't her fault that he had died, it tore her apart that he had died blaming her. She mourned her mother, whose bitterness was destroying her. Deborah decided she could let her mother blame her. She prayed that her mother would find Jesus and finally find peace and love and joy. She prayed for truth to win out at Jacob's trial. She prayed that he would be protected when he served his sentence. By the time she finished, she was filled with peace, knowing God would always be with her.

She also prayed for Ash, not really knowing what to pray for. "Lord, give me a chance to talk to him. Bring him to me." The ground inclined a bit more than she expected and suddenly Deborah was on the ground in terrible pain. She could not think and she could barely move. Her finger mashed the emergency call button on her phone and she slipped into unconsciousness.

The smell of disinfectant and the cacophonous sounds of voices, beeps and tones invaded the dark silence. Deborah opened her eyes to painful bright lights as the world came swimming back to her. She was in a hospital bed. Her head throbbed and her chest stabbed her with each breath she took. Her eyes adjusted to the brightness, and it became slightly less painful. She looked around to see Catherine sitting in a bedside chair, dozing. It made her smile to know her friend cared so much about her.

Then Oliver, Simon, and Ash walked into the room. Simon spoke, "Mom, we're here to bring you down to eat. Ash is going to stay with Deborah."

As Catherine woke up, it seemed the group noticed Deborah was awake at the same time. Simon, Oliver, and Catherine all spoke at the same time. "Deborah! Oh, it's good to see those eyes open!" "Thank God, you're okay!" "Welcome back to the world of the living!"

Simon said, "I'll go get let the nurse know." He left the room and passed Ash, who stood in the doorway. His face was joy, relief, and trepidation rolled into one expression.

Deborah tried to sit up but pain wracked her body when she moved.

"No, don't try to sit up yet," Catherine said. "Let the nurse help you."

"What happened?" Deborah hated to sound clichéd, but she wanted to know. She looked to Ash for a moment, wishing he would come hold her and kiss her. When he didn't move, she turned to Catherine.

"Dear, you fell in the woods. What were you doing out there in the mud? You hit your head and got a concussion, and bruised a rib and your back. You are quite 'banged up,' as the doctor put it. Is that a medical term?"

Deborah again looked at Ash, wondering how he was there. He finally spoke. "Catherine called me. I hope that's alright. I couldn't stay away."

Deborah could barely contain her thoughts. How could he say something like that, when staying away was exactly what he had done for months? She was about to answer when the nurse came in.

"Miss Wade, I'm going to examine you now." She turned to the roomful of visitors, "Will you please wait outside for a few minutes?" They complied, and she examined Deborah and asked her a series of questions. An IV in Deborah's arm began to drip painkillers, which gave everything a nice happy glow. "I've called the doctor and he will be by this evening," the nurse told Deborah, adjusting her position in the bed. "Just press this button if you need anything. I don't want you in pain, and please, do not get out of this bed without a nurse or a nursing assistant to help you. Is that clear?"

"Yes. Thank you." Deborah could barely move; she doubted she was going to try and venture out of the bed. The pain medicine worked its magic over her and made her head float a little as it replaced the sharp pain with tolerable twinges.

Glancing at a clock, Deborah found she had been unconscious for fourteen hours, and could only imagine how worried everyone had been. For being out so long, she was surprised at how very tired she was. The family came back in, and Deborah told them, "Go home and rest, or at least go get something to eat."

Oliver answered her. "We'll go down and eat. You rest. We'll be back shortly."

"I'm going to stay with her," Ash looked toward Deborah for her permission and sat in the bedside chair.

The Copelands left them alone. Deborah was so tired, but she wanted to talk to Ash. He took her hand. "Go to sleep. We have plenty of time to talk later."

How did he always know what she was thinking? She drifted easily off to sleep as she heard his voice, "I'm so sorry. I didn't know. I'm so sorry."

BRAND NEW DAY

Deborah had been home from the hospital for a week. Catherine insisted she take a room in the manor until she was healed, and refused to let her lift a finger. It seemed Elsa was her private maid, and she would be held responsible for any work Deborah did, including pouring a glass of water or buttering a piece of toast. Deborah acquiesced for the moment, but she was hoping she would soon be ready to go back home.

Elsa filled Deborah's nearly empty tea cup and handed her the requested copy of *Jane Eyre* from the cottage. "Thank you, Elsa," she said, dutifully drinking the tea. The woman's attentiveness was appreciated but almost unnerving to someone who was not used to having a person serve her every need.

Deborah put off her boredom by delving into *Jane Eyre* and, as always, hoped the heroine would see Mr. Rochester had done the things he had out of love and duty. Her ringing phone pulled her from Thornfield Hall and brought her back to Cumberland Manor. It was Ash.

Deborah took a deep breath and answered. "Hello."

"Deborah, I have no right to ask, but I need to see you. May I come by and talk?" He sounded so hopeful.

Whatever this conversation held, Deborah knew it needed to happen. She had been praying it would, even though she wasn't sure if she would like the results. "Yes, of course. I want to see you, Ash."

"I'm near Cumberland, about ten minutes away. May I come now?"

"Yes, yes. Please do." Deborah hung up the phone, her heart leaping at the idea of seeing Ash. "Elsa, I need help. I'm going to change my clothes. Can you clean this up and arrange coffee for Asher Levine and tea for me in the sitting room? He'll be here in about ten minutes."

Elsa helped Deborah up the stairs, set her up to wash her face, called Ian to arrange the trays, and returned to take care of Deborah. She brushed her hair, helped her apply some makeup, and helped her get dressed. When they came downstairs, Ash was already in the sitting room. He saw Deborah and stood up with a look of expectant bliss on his expressive face.

Deborah was struck by his handsome features. His dark curly hair, olive skin, and bright eyes nearly melted her heart, but she was resolved to speak her piece. She had so many questions, but all that came out was, "I'm really glad you came." Her voice was reserved as she held on to her feelings like a buoy in a turbulent ocean. Her knees wobbling a little, she eased herself into a chair.

As Ash was about to answer, Ian arrived with a tray holding a coffee urn, a tea pot, sugar, cream, two cups and an array of cakes. Ian began to pour, but Ash took over. "I've got it, thank you," he said. He still knew exactly how Deborah liked her tea, adding more sugar than most people would find appropriate. Ian and Elsa left the room. Asher finally felt free to speak, and speak he did. His words tumbled out. "I am so sorry, Deborah. You chose Jacob and I wanted you to be happy. I was in love with you and you were in love with him. I didn't want to get in the way of your happiness."

Deborah lost her grip on the buoy. "You were supposed to love me! How can you call leaving me to a child molester love? I was all alone. I needed you and you weren't there." She let her anger steel her against the tears that threatened to break the dam of her heart.

"I didn't know he was a child molester." Ash's voice was becoming louder. "You know that I didn't know. Neither of us knew. He fooled everyone. You were in love, and I wanted you to be happy. I left so I wouldn't interfere. I suffered without you!"

"You suffered? What about me? I suffered, too! I wouldn't have fallen in love with Jacob if I had thought you loved me. You never showed me an inkling of anything, and then you just gave up! If you loved me, wouldn't you have seen who he was, when I was blind to it? Do you know the attacks I had to put up with? Do you know the turmoil I went through thinking of those poor children?"

Ash stood up and stepped closer to Deborah. "He deceived all of us. He is a liar and I fell for his lies as much as you did. I thought I was leaving you to a good man. I thought I was giving you what you wanted, what you told me you wanted. I never would have gone if I had imagined that he was lying. Do you think I didn't miss you every single day?"

Now Deborah was standing too. She jabbed her finger at him. "You thought I wanted some heartless monster? You left. I needed you! I wanted you! I was left with nothing. I cried until there was nothing left to cry. I missed you I nearly called you a hundred times. I begged God to send you to me. Do you know what I went through? Do you even care? Jacob hurt me, he nearly destroyed me. But you hurt me much worse. How cou..."

All of a sudden, Ash's arms were around her. He pulled her close and held on to her tightly. She struggled against him, but his arms remained firm. She could not wriggle out of them. As Deborah inhaled to continue her tirade in defiance of his grip, he leaned down, put his lips on her forehead and kissed her softly. She tried to push him away, but his arms did not relinquish her. Finally, she sagged into his embrace and wrapped her arms around him. Her anger flowed out of her in tears. Her knees had given out and she was leaning on him, so he lifted her and carried her to the couch. He set her gently on the cushions, kissed her forehead once more, and gave her a handkerchief. Then he poured her a fresh cup of tea, bringing the hot elixir to her and sitting by her side. "I am so sorry. Please forgive me. I love you desperately and completely."

Deborah took a sip of the soothing liquid,

set the cup down and leaned against him and cried tears both happy and sad. "Yes, always, yes." They sat without talking for five minutes while Deborah cried into Ash's shirt. Then she spoke into his heart, "I love you. I have since the moment I met you. I love you."

PLAN ON FOREVER

Deborah held the envelope in her hand, another letter she had written to her mother, unopened and marked Return to Sender. "It's okay," she thought. "I'll keep praying. God told me to forgive you, and that's exactly what I've done, even if you don't know about it." She tossed the unopened letter in the trash and left to get in her car.

Her first stop was Bierman's Boutique, a shop in Belle Cay that specialized in custom-designed dresses and was popular for weddings. Denise was shopping for her wedding dress, and Deborah had volunteered to come along. The joy of that particular errand helped keep her from dwelling on the unopened letter. Her mother could go on stewing in her own bitterness; Deborah was watching her friends get married and come alive and change for the better.

She pulled up to the shop and met Denise, who was waiting outside. "I got here a little early," said the doctor. "I can't believe this is happening. Thanks for being with me today."

Deborah hugged her friend. "It makes me happy to see you so happy." She also imagined being here for herself someday, having Jackie and Denise by her side to help her design her dress. They rang the bell for the shop.

Denise rang the shop's bell, and a refined young woman with a bun of dark gold hair answered the door. "Please come in. I'm Karen Bierman." She stood aside and motioned them in to the shop. On one side a few dresses hung on a rack, and nearby were mannequins sporting gowns. One wall had a dressing room, while the center of the room sported a small pedestal in front of a couch and several chairs. The other side of the room had a desk and chairs next to a bookcase, with several books of drawings and photos of dresses.

Karen led the women to the desk. "Congratulations, Dr. Woods. I'm so happy you're going to give me the chance to help you design your dress. Do you have any ideas about what you're hoping for?"

"I do have some ideas, but none are really concrete. I spend a great deal of my time working and I don't know what's fashionable or what styles work best for me." Denise pulled a little notebook from her pocket. "I would love as much input as you want to give."

"Great!" said Karen. "I can help you." She went to the shelves and retrieved a book, then returned to the desk and pulled a sketch pad from a drawer. "You have a lovely figure and I think it would be best accentuated by a twenties-inspired dress. It will make you appear taller and flatter your figure." She opened the book to show her some pictures of similar dresses. "Do you like these?"

Denise looked at the dresses. "They're so elegant. I love the lacework on this one." She pointed at one then moved to another. "The shape of this one is nice. I think I would like it to hang a bit closer to my body. I don't want it to cling at all though."

The designer happily sketched something. "Something like this?" The dress came in ever so slightly at the waist. "We can make a lace layer over the top."

"Yes! That's beautiful. How about the length? I'd love it to go to the floor. Does that work?"

"Okay." Karen drew quickly and presented her next sketch. "How's this?"

Denise was thrilled. She had been searching for a dress for weeks and had not considered designing one until Catherine suggested it. Karen took out a new page and sketched a final design for the dress. Then they went through the same process with a veil.

Deborah was very impressed with the entire design. "Mrs. Bierman, the dress is better than anything we've seen so far. Thank you."

"My pleasure," said the gracious woman. "Now, are you interested in having me design the bridal party dresses?"

Denise brightened, "Yes. I'm just going to have one attendant." She turned to Deborah. "I would be grateful if you would be my maid of honor. Is that what they call it when there is only one? You mean so much to both Simon and me."

Deborah blushed. "I would love to."

The three women spent some time designing a dress for Deborah that would complement Denise's dress yet be unique to her. In the end, they chose a knee-length dress. It would be pale coral with deep blue beaded lace overlay. It was the sort of dress Deborah saw in her mind's eye when she read about the elegant parties in *The Great Gatsby*.

Before they left, they made an appointment for Oliver and Simon to have custom tuxedos made. Karen would ensure that they matched the theme without revealing the wedding dress to the groom.

Donna Campbell

TAKE ME HOME COUNTRY ROADS

Deborah and Ash stood hand in hand in a cemetery in Ocoee, Florida, one thousand one hundred and eighty-three miles from Belle Cay, Connecticut. Deborah read her father's gravestone. "Mark Wade, Beloved Husband, Friend to the Community." A tear escaped her eye. "That is how my mother remembers him. That is how he wanted to be known. Maybe he wasn't a beloved father, but once I had some good memories of him. Before I saw him with Daisy, I could think of the times he let himself be my dad, the times he tickled me and told me corny jokes. Once we went to pick up take-out for dinner to surprise my mom, and on the way home he bought ice cream cones. We had to eat the ice creams before we got home so she didn't know. It was our treat just for us. Dessert before supper." She was smiling. "I never would have believed he was capable of the things he did, if I hadn't seen it with my own eyes. Of course my mother couldn't bring herself to believe it."

Ash squeezed her hand. "That is a lot of mercy. I'm proud of you."

"Now," said Deborah, "comes the hard

part. I need to go see my mom. And I need to go alone."

"We'll go back to the hotel and have a bite to eat, and then you can leave me there while you do this. You won't be alone. I'm with you and so is God." He did an impression of E.T. "Right here." Ash took his finger and pressed it to her chest. Then he kissed her forehead, which she always loved.

She laughed and gave Ash a hug. A weed growing from the gravesite caught her attention and she knelt down at the grave and pulled it from the ground. "Goodbye, dad." She stood and walked out of the cemetery with Ash.

Two hours later Deborah stood in front of the small house where she had grown up. She longed to sit on the porch swing again, talking about hopes and dreams with Jackie. She yearned to once more enjoy watermelon and barbecue in the yard for some festive occasion. She wished for one more day of lying out in the sun in the makeshift paradise of the front yard, sitting on the old lawn chair with her toes dipped in the child's pool and the radio playing the top forty countdown. Yet the front door loomed over all her memories. With quivering knees she stepped up onto the porch, took a deep breath and knocked.

Her mother answered the door. Eileen's long dark hair was now short and peppered with gray. Her face held more wrinkles, and her eyes were wearier. "Yes?" she said. "May I help you?" She looked at the woman on the porch for a moment before recognizing her daughter. Eileen went pale. Her face became a steel mask, and she turned around and walked inside the house, leaving the door open.

Unsure what she should do, Deborah followed her in. She wanted to say something, but felt God urging her, *Just wait; be silent for now.* So Deborah stood in the living room of her mother's house, looking at Eileen Wade's back.

Eileen didn't cry. She just stood there with her back to Deborah. It seemed the silence would stretch on forever. Had it been one minute, or five, or ten? Finally the silence was broken. "Why did you come here?" Eileen's voice was bitterly cold.

Deborah stepped closer to her mother. "I'm sorry." She offered no excuses or explanations. "I'm so sorry."

Eileen kept her back to her daughter. "What does that do for me? Big deal. You're sorry. It's too late for sorry."

"I know. But I am. I just want you to know. You're my mother. Nothing will ever change that. I love you."

Eileen's back shook with silent cries. Without turning around she walked into the kitchen. Deborah wasn't sure what to do. Should she leave? Follow her mother into the kitchen? Stay where she was?

Follow her. Pursue this.

Deborah went into the kitchen and saw her mother with her head down on the table. Deborah didn't speak. For lack of anything else to do, she quietly made a pot of coffee; the cups were still in the same place and her mother's favorite mug sat in its usual spot. She pulled it and another mug out and poured the hot coffee into both of them, setting them on the table and sat down next to her mother. "You've been working hard. Have a cup o' joseph." A cup of joseph had been a joke between her parents when they wanted fancy coffee.

Eileen sat up and took a sip of the dark liquid. "Thank you."

They talked. The conversation was careful, hesitant, and trivial. Deborah asked questions about her mother's jobs and friends. There was no mention of her father, the trial, or anything close to it. Eileen was working as a dental hygienist during the day for a company she liked. In the evenings she worked as a cashier in a thrift store. She was considering dating a man who had asked her out.

Deborah in turn told her a little about Ash. It was a beginning, and it was more than Deborah could have hoped for. When the pot was empty, Deborah stood to leave. "Mom, here's my number. If you want to talk again, call me. I would love it. If not, that's up to you. I'm okay as long as I know you're okay."

They didn't hug. They said goodbye with a small smile and half a nod. As Deborah left, her heart felt lighter than it had in months. She called Jackie to make sure they were still meeting for dinner, started the rental car, and drove back to Ash.

Donna Campbell

WITH A LITTLE HELP FROM MY FRIENDS

Deborah and Ash met Jackie and her husband Ed at a restaurant on Cocoa Beach, an hour outside of Ocoee. The kitschy décor and beach atmosphere belied the delicious food the restaurant offered; the Tidal Pool was renowned in the area for its tropical seafood and gourmet tapas. This restaurant had been a favorite of Deborah's since she was a teenager when she and Jackie would go to the beach at least once a week from February to October.

It had been so long since she had seen Jackie in person, but there was no missing her beautiful friend. Jackie still had hair as white blond as she had when she was a child. She was a towhead then and a towhead now. Her fair skin was freckled from years of enjoying life in the sun, and her blue eyes sparkled with the joy of her life. Jackie rushed to Deborah and embraced her for a full minute. She reluctantly released her and held her hand toward her husband. "This is Ed, my hubby."

Deborah knew Ed, but only through the

many letters and phone calls she shared with Jackie. He was a large man in every way. Had he been wearing tall boots and a flannel shirt he might have been Paul Bunyan. "Ed, it is so nice to finally meet you in person." He gripped her hand and gave it a firm shake. Deborah turned to Ash. "This is Ash Levine, my boyfriend. Ash, this is Jackie, my best friend in the entire world besides you. And this is Ed, her husband and the man that saved her life."

"So glad to meet you," said Ash, shaking both their hands. "Jackie, thank you for being there for Deborah even across so many miles."

They were led to a table decorated with plastic palm fronds and beach umbrellas. "So tell me, Ed," Ash said, "how is it that you saved Jackie's life?"

Ed looked up from his menu "Well, I was there for her when she needed me." He didn't elaborate.

Jackie spoke up then with a ten-minute story of how she met Ed, who had rescued her from the unwanted advances of a customer at her convenience store job years earlier. He had waited around throughout her shift, and when she got off work, she almost got into his car because it was the same year, make, model, and color as her own. Jackie had a flair for turning almost any memory into a side-splitting comedic tale. That story led to one after another with plenty of rabbit trails for philosophy and deep conversation. It was as if Deborah and Jackie saw one another every day. There was no need to catch-up or explain things.

A couple of hours later, the waitress was cleaning away the dessert dishes and pouring fresh drinks for the table. Ash said, "I'm really glad to be visiting Florida. Your hospitality has made me feel like family. Thank you. I want to return the favor." He pulled a small blue box from his jacket. He glanced at Deborah but then returned his attention to Ed and Jackie. "I want you to come to Connecticut and join us for our wedding." He finally turned his attention to Deborah, who quickly closed her agape mouth. "That is, if you will marry me." He opened the box to reveal a lovely little pear-shaped diamond on a simple gold setting.

Deborah had expected they would get married. They had even talked about their wedding as Denise and Simon planned theirs, but she had not expected him to ask her tonight. "Yes! Undeniably, unequivocally, and unconditionally yes!"

Ash placed the ring on Deborah's finger, accompanied by Ed and Jackie's cheering. When the staff heard the commotion, several of them appeared. The waitress set four glasses of sparkling wine in front of them. "Congratulations!" she said with happy tears brimming from her eyes.

Jackie raised her glass. "To family, new and old, here, wherever, now, and forever."

"Here, here!" was the resounding response from throughout The Tidal Pool.

GOING HOME

The ringing phone woke Deborah from a peaceful sleep. For a moment she was not aware of her surroundings, and her awakening brain reminded her she was in a hotel in Florida. She reached for the phone automatically checking the time and the caller ID. It was nine-thirty in the morning and the call was from Anna Ruiz. All her peace was vanquished in a moment as her stomach and heart did a gymnastic routine within in her chest. "Hello," she said hesitantly, knowing the news would be about the Jacob's trial. She had specifically chosen to come to Florida to be away from it, once cleared from having to testify.

"Good Morning, Miss Wade, I'm sorry to wake you," came the composed voice of the detective.

"I had to wake up anyway, to answer the phone." Deborah covered her anticipation with the old family joke.

"I wanted to let you know that Jacob has been found guilty of all charges. The prosecutor wanted to call you and let you know, but I offered to make the call. I think he would have waited until he had a free moment and that may not have been for a week."

There was silence as Deborah tried to collect her thoughts and feelings. She willed her stomach to stop doing flips and coaxed her heart to slow its rapid beat. She had no words and no idea what response she should give. "When will he be sentenced?"

"He already has. He tried to make a plea bargain, but Judge Peterman did not accept the deal, and gave him thirty years."

Deborah's heart froze and now she had to persuade it to start up again. Thirty years; he would be in his sixties when he finally stepped out of the prison. How was she supposed to feel? Should she be elated, cheering like the people she saw on the news? She wasn't happy, nor was she sorrowful over the verdict. More than anything, she was simply uncertain. The injustice had already happened; justice could only be simulated now, and she supposed it had been. "Thank you, Detective. I appreciate the call." Hanging up, she stretched, prayed, and let God put her stomach and heart back into right working order before she called Ash's room to prepare for the trip home.

Deborah sat down in the small airplane seat. She had not looked forward to going to Florida, and though parts had been difficult, overall it had been tremendous. She had said goodbye to her father. A relationship with her mother was a new and hopeful prospect. Jacob was well on his way to being a part of her past. She had seen Jackie and had even found time to enjoy being a tourist. Her eyes drifted down to the ring on her finger. It felt as if it belonged there, not too heavy, uncomfortable or even strange. It was right where it should be. She was so glad that Ash had convinced her to go.

Her mother had not called her yet, but whatever Eileen Wade chose to do, Deborah was okay with it. She had let her mother know she cared, and was willing to wait for her to heal some more. She hoped her mother would heal and reconcile, but she was leaving it to God.

"Are you going to miss home?" Ash asked as he leaned over to check her seatbelt.

"I can't miss home as long as I'm with you." She leaned over and kissed his cheek. "Besides, if any place is my home right now, it's Belle Cay and Cumberland Manor. One day soon, it will be whatever place you and I choose to live. I know that seems a bit trite, but I really feel that way. I never understood it before. You are my home, Asher Levine."

On the plane they talked over their wedding plans. Ash would ask Jim Ramirez to be his best man. Jackie had already agreed to be the maid of honor. They would find special places for Simon, Oliver, Frank, Brian, Christian, Dave, and Denise. If they had them all as attendants, the wedding could quickly get out of hand. Asher had six brothers and sisters to consider as well. Deborah would ask Catherine to walk her down the aisle, and would also ask Sarah to be her flower girl.

They decided to wait until after Simon and Denise's wedding next week to announce their engagement. That was just one more thing to love about Ash; he didn't want to steal the attention from his new friends and family.

Epsilon was gaining a little more following. Deborah had even heard *Too Far the Distance* on the radio in Florida, and it might be too easy to let the spotlight turn from Denise and Simon to Ash and Deborah.

I HOPE

Denise, Catherine, and Deborah worked together to finish the wedding invitations. Deborah wrote out the addresses, Catherine sealed the envelopes, and Denise applied the appropriate postage. Deborah addressed the last envelope to her mother, then sealed it and stamped it herself. She held it in her hands, hesitant about adding it to the pile. Five months had passed since she had talked to her mother. If she mailed the invitation, it gave her mother another chance to reject her.

If you invite her, it will give you both another chance to make peace.

Deborah just loved how God spoke to her. It had surprised her to find out that not everyone had similar conversations with Him. Some people heard Him differently, others didn't listen, and many had not found it as easy as she had to simply have a conversation with God. Denise had told her it was a gift, and it was one Deborah was more than happy to enjoy. She put the thick cream envelope on the pile to be mailed. "It's yours, Lord."

"I hope she comes." Catherine hugged Deborah. "Shall we make an afternoon of mailing them? I think we could all use a pedicure."

"That sounds wonderful," said Denise, "but I have so much to do to finish the house." Simon had bought Denise a mansion a few miles from Cumberland. She was busy furnishing it, hiring staff, and turning the house they had dubbed Copeland Park into a home.

"What is it you need to do today?" asked Deborah.

"I'm meeting the designer to furnish the bedrooms. I think that's the final step. It should take about two more weeks and all the workers, movers, and painters will be gone." She lifted her glass of cucumber water and took a swig. "I don't know if I'm nesting or what, but I can barely wait to finish, and I keep finding more to do." She placed her hand on the barely noticeable bulge on her abdomen.

"I don't want you to overdo it, dear." Catherine spoke with her regal authority.

"I'm not overdoing it. I need to remain active and healthy for this baby and Simon. Besides, I had no idea how much would be involved in becoming a wife. I don't have the luxury of taking a bit of down time."

Deborah interjected. "Then I propose we go get pedicures tomorrow. In fact, Denise, I insist. I'll mail these myself right now. You go home and meet your designer, and Catherine, you are supposed to meet Elana Arcola in an hour at the Belle Cay Hotel. Karen Bierman is coming by this afternoon at four."

Catherine assented. "Thank you. What will I do without you?"

"Let's not worry about that. You will be just fine. We all will." Deborah hid the hint of a tear at the thought of leaving her family behind when she got married and moved in with Ash. "Okay, I'm off. I'll see you later." She gave the women each a peck on the cheek, took the pile of invitations and left for the post office.

Donna Campbell

HOMEWARD BOUND

"There are times when things seem to work out so ideally that a person can only call it providence. This is one of those times." Allen Kennedy seemed as excited as a schoolboy. He and his wife Annette and had been doing premarital counseling for Deborah and Ash. During the counseling, the issue of where the couple would live had come up. Deborah wanted to stay in Connecticut, close to her new family and her church. Ash was based in New York for Epsilon. Allen had what he hoped was a solution.

"Our music and youth minister is leaving to become a missionary in Haiti. We are in need of a new one. Ash, if you're interested in applying for the job and you meet the requirements, it may be an answer to all our prayers. You could live here, travel with Epsilon as needed, and go to New York whenever you are required to. I'm not making any promises; I have to check your background and references, and I need to know that you are right for the job. But I do think this is going to work out." He paused. "If, that is, you're interested."

Ash had told Deborah many times that he

missed being a music minister, and seemed to agree with Allen's idea about all of this being divine intervention. "Yes! I would love to apply for the job. Thanks."

Allen gave Ash a thick envelope. "Here's the application. The sooner you fill it out, the sooner the process will begin. You've been attending church here for a while, and people like you. If you meet the prerequisites, I don't foresee an issue passing the committee approval."

Deborah and Ash left the pastor's office in such a giddy mood that they began house hunting immediately. Belle Cay was beyond their means, but Belleshore was not. If the imminent approach of the wedding had felt real before, passing houses and writing down addresses and phone numbers from For Sale signs made it even more real. Soon Deborah would be furnishing a house and decorating a baby's room.

"It does all seem too perfect to be true," she said.

"It is true. If I get this job, we will live somewhere here. If I don't, we still will because I know now I don't need to live in Manhattan. We can live anywhere and I can still do my job. Besides, I checked the job qualifications and I more than meet them."

"You do?" Deborah nearly squealed with joy.

"Yep. I told you a long time ago that I have a doctorate in theology, and my bachelor's was in music. You know I already have experience as a music minister, and that job often coupled up with the youth ministry. You know, I'm practically a rock star." His eyes twinkled with the exaggeration. "My time with Epsilon has given me a lot of time to talk with kids, hurting kids, excited kids, and every kind you can think of. I really love kids. I love that they have all this potential and they only need a little boost to help them get closer to it."

"Could I call you Doctor Levine?" Deborah had forgotten she was marrying a scholar. If she held a doctorate in anything she would likely have had her degree emblazoned across her forehead or chest, but it had not occurred to Ash to boast about his accomplishments.

"You technically could, but yeah, I think I prefer Pastor Levine, or just plain Ash. I think my favorite name will be Mr. Levine when I can call you Mrs. Levine."

"That's my favorite name by far." She snuggled into his side and allowed herself to dream of houses and babies.

A month later, Asher received the news that he would be the new Music and Youth Pastor for Belleshore Community Fellowship. The couple wasted no time in making an appointment with a real estate agent. Deborah found a card for Tracy Henderson of Belleshore Realty, Inc. Ash called and made the appointment to speak with her.

Ash and Deborah entered the offices of Belleshore Realty holding hands and filled with the expectant hope of their future. But when the agent came out to introduce herself, Deborah felt her hope dissipate. The woman had not uttered a word; she stood motionless as her polite salesperson mask was replaced with stone cold hate. Deborah had not connected the name Tracy Henderson to Michelle, the mother of one of Jacob's victims.

"I can't help you. No. I could, but I will not have you living here in my town. I won't help you. Goodbye." Tracy Henderson began to turn away and retreat to the inner office she had emerged from.

"Ash, this is Tracy Henderson, Michelle's mother. Let's go." Deborah was devastated. She wanted to leave the building as quickly as possible. She took Ash's hand to tug him toward the door.

But Ash stood his ground. "Mrs. Henderson, I know you want to blame someone, but Deborah is not responsible for what happened to your daughter. What happened to her is beyond horrible. It isn't your fault and it isn't Michelle's either. It is fully and completely Jacob Armel's fault. He is serving thirty years in prison for his crimes. He will face God at the end of his days. That doesn't change what he did. It doesn't make up for it. But I don't want you to keep punishing yourself or Deborah for the evil that he committed. Hasn't Jacob done enough to hurt Michelle and your family?"

Deborah was in awe of the man she loved. She expected Mrs. Henderson to begin yelling or slap her again, but she didn't. She remained still and quiet for a few minutes then she spoke through tears. "Please wait here, while I find another agent to help you." She walked into the back offices.

Deborah and Ash sat down. "You are amazing! Thank you." Deborah had told Asher about their last confrontation. He had both stood up for Deborah and showed such kindness, even mercy, to Mrs. Henderson that Deborah loved him even more.

Ash winked at Deborah. "I know, I am purty darned good, ain't I? You know, I can't imagine how she feels. I'm sure she believes she failed at her job of protecting her daughter. She's angry, she's hurt, and if she can punish you, then it makes her feel a little bit better. She needs love and compassion. She needs to heal."

"You are purty darned good, Asher Levine, not to mention just plain purty." His compassion astounded her.

Soon after, they were looking at a computer with Fannie Hyman, another agent in the office. They were talking about what they wanted in a house, how much they could afford, and other details that reignited Deborah's excitement. They made a list of suitable houses and arranged to go see them.

At first each house looked perfect, but then Deborah would see something that suggested a cracked foundation, leaks in the basement, or too little space. It was becoming tiresome. She was ready to pack it in for the day and look at the last two houses another time. Her feet ached and her mind was tired, and she still had a pile of work waiting her for on her desk at Cumberland, plus wedding details to finalize. Ash persisted, though. "It's just two more, darling. You can manage it."

The next house had three bedrooms and two stories, with a basement that had been converted to a one-bedroom apartment. Although Deborah didn't love the steep entryway, she liked the rest of the floor plan. There were no detectable leaks and no cracks to be seen.

"The asking price is above what we're looking to pay," Ash pointed out.

"That's true," Fannie conceded, "but I don't think it will hurt you to make an offer. I'm almost certain the seller intentionally asked for more than he thought he would get. I have to say, though, he might just get what he wants if you wait too long. There is a beautiful forest that meets the property line back there." Fannie had led the couple outside. "The schools here are top notch and within walking distance, and the neighborhood is very close-knit. This house is going to get snatched up."

Although Deborah wasn't a fan of a sales pitch, she had begun to see the house as nearly perfect. They could fix the entry stairs, or she could get used to them. She squeezed Ash's hand twice, their secret signal that one or the other wanted to move forward on the house. He squeezed it back in answer, but said, "Let's look at the last house on the list."

In the car following Fannie Hyman, the two talked and decided on what they would offer. "I think it will be too low," Ash said, "but

I just have a good feeling. Plus I don't want to pay more than that. If God wants us to have that house, then we will, and if not then a better house will come along." Deborah loved Ash's faith.

The next house was within their price range, but it was a cramped two-bedroom on a main road. Deborah knew she was finding all its faults only because she wanted the previous house so much. At the end of tour, Ash instructed Fannie to put in an offer for the house they both hoped would be theirs one day soon.

WE ARE FAMILY

Michael and Eva Levine met their son and his fiancée at the airport. Eva hugged Deborah before she even looked at her son. "Oh, honey! Welcome to the family!" The slightly plump redhead took Deborah's face in her hands. "Oh, so pretty! Asher, why didn't you tell us she was so pretty?" She kissed each cheek, then turned to her son, hugging him fiercely before Deborah had a chance to reply.

Mr. Levine took Deborah's hand and kissed her forehead just the way Ash tended to do. "Deborah, welcome," he said warmly.

"Thank you both! It's so nice to meet you." said Deborah. She had never met parents like his before, and she was certain she already loved them. Ash and Deborah followed his parents out to the car.

Eva's arm remained around her son; there was no hiding her love and pride for him. "You must be starving! I have supper ready and waiting for us."

Asher and Michael loaded the luggage into the trunk of the sedan and then the four got into the car and headed to his parents' home in Breakneck, Tennessee. Over the hour-long drive from the airport, Eva asked Deborah question after question. Such a barrage of questions could easily have felt like an inquisition, but the warmth Eva radiated made it clear she actually cared to know the answers because she cared to know Deborah. By the time they reached the house, Deborah had shared more of her personal story than she had ever planned on sharing with the Levines.

While the men carried the bags into the house, Eva put her arms around Deborah. "Dear, I'm so glad you're not alone anymore. You're my daughter now. Nothing will change that."

Michael seconded his wife. "Yes, we're family now. And you know? I wouldn't give up hope for your mother either. God is bigger than we can consider. Nothing is impossible with Him."

"Ash, take Deborah to the girls' old room, and you can set yourself up in your old room. I'm serving up dinner in ten minutes, so hurry and wash up." Mrs. Levine was already in the kitchen preparing to serve up the delicious-smelling food.

Deborah walked up the stairs behind Ash as he told her about each picture on the wall. There was a large family portrait, showing a gawky fourteen-year-old Ash, as well as individual portraits of each of the Levine children. "This one is Nya, the baby of the family. This is Nathaniel. Here's Jen. Then

James and John; they're twins. You already know me. And last but not least, my big sister Katie. Nya and Nate are both in college now, and everyone else is planning on coming by tomorrow."

"Wow. How can I remember everyone?"

"No worries. You'll remember... eventually. Tomorrow it's just five of my siblings, three spouses and six kids. No big deal " He laughed and gave her a quick kiss on her forehead.

Dinner turned out to be chicken and dumplings. "This could be the best chicken and dumplings I have ever had," Deborah told them, wondering if they would judge her for requesting a second helping.

"Oh, thank you!" Eva replied. "It's an old family recipe." Without asking she filled Deborah's bowl with more of the scrumptious dinner.

After supper Mr. Levine took his son into the den for a pre-wedding father and son talk. Deborah went into the kitchen with Eva, and the two cleaned up together. Deborah had her chance to ask questions about Ash and his childhood.

"My son is a bona fide genius! He graduated high school when he was sixteen years old." Eva gleamed with pride. "He chose to use his gifts to do what he loves. Have you heard his music? Oh! Of course you have. And what he loves more than anything else is Jesus. He uses his gifts for Jesus and to make people happy. I'm so lucky he's my son."

"I'm lucky he's going to be my husband,"

said Deborah dreamily.

"You are blessed, but I can see my Asher is the lucky one to have you." She handed Deborah a wet dish to dry. "Do you know that Jewish tradition says you and the person God chose for you used to be one spirit? But you were torn apart into two souls, perfectly matched for one another. You've spent your life up to now searching for your other half. The Jewish people see this as an analogy of man's separation from God when the Temple was destroyed."

The pile of wet dishes grew as Deborah held one wet plate and her towel still in mid-air. The story enraptured her. Eva picked up a second towel and began drying, which reminded Deborah to continue the job as well. Eva resumed the story. "Christians know that the marriage represents our reconciliation to God through Jesus Christ in the marriage supper of the Lamb. And so marriage also represents the two halves of your spirits reuniting into one soul through Christ."

"Amazing! I have never heard that kind of perspective before. It's beautiful. Ash is my soul mate. I felt it the moment I met him. It took me a little while to recognize it, though."

Eva kissed Deborah's head. "But you finally did. That is something I am very happy about."

Asher and Deborah were only able to stay in Tennessee for three days, because Ash had to leave on tour. Those three days were blissful for Deborah, who by the end of the trip was calling Mr. and Mrs. Levine "Mom" and "Dad." She wasn't sure she would ever get all the brothers, sisters, husbands, wives, and kids straight, but Ash had assured her she would.

Donna Campbell

LESS THAN WHOLE

Life was moving quickly. Deborah Wade would soon be Deborah Levine, the wife of a youth pastor and music minister and bassist in a rock band. She would soon be living in her own home with her husband. Deborah had been very surprised when their initial low offer for the house had been accepted, but she quickly caught herself. Why should she be surprised that God had answered their prayers?

Her family would begin with Ash, but instead of growing smaller, it was only growing bigger. Once she had been alone. Now she had Asher, the Levines, the Copelands, and Belleshore Community Fellowship. She wanted her mother to be part of the family as well. Although she herself once again considered Eileen family, she wasn't sure how Eileen felt.

"Lord, heal my mother. Love her. Bless her," she said as she cleaned the cottage. It had become an often-repeated prayer. Deborah's own struggles and pain had made her forget the love she once felt for her mother, and she was trying hard to remember it. It was slowly dawning on her that she had never considered the way her mother had been hurt by men, or how her mother had felt about what happened to her father. Eileen was blind to her husband's actions because she needed to be. Deborah had only thought about how her parents had hurt her and not how damaged they were or how she had hurt them. She never regretted calling the police over what her father had done to Daisy, but she wondered if she might have tried harder not to alienate her parents. In a way it didn't matter anymore. It was in the past and couldn't be changed, but she had done what she could to shape the future into a brighter one.

Elsa knocked on the door and said, "Miss Wade, I have some mail for you."

The mail for the cottage went to the main house, and Deborah normally just got it when she was there. She couldn't imagine what could make Elsa bring her mail over now. She opened the door and greeted the bright young woman, relieved to see a happy expression on her face. "Is it good news?" She asked as she held her hand out for the promised mail.

"Well, I don't know, but I do know you've been waiting for this." Elsa gave Deborah a small pile of RSVPs to add to the many she had already received.

The top envelope was from Eileen Wade. Deborah set the rest down on the coffee table and held the one from her mother in both hands. Her stomach was tight. When she opened this, it would either be another rejection or another step toward healing.

"I had better get back to work, Miss Wade," said Elsa, though she made no move to leave.

"No, please stay. I'm not sure I can open this by myself. I'd like you to stay." Deborah moved to the couch to sit down.

Elsa followed her. She was nearly as curious as Deborah. She sat down and took Deborah's hand. "You can do this. It is already written. All you have to do is read it."

Deborah opened the RSVP and slipped it from the envelope with her eyes closed. She breathed a prayer and opened her eyes. She read it out loud. "I will not be attending." Deborah's heart sank. There was a small note written below. *"I'm sorry. I cannot afford the time off work. Congratulations."* Deborah clutched the card. "Well, at least she responded. That's more than she might've done in the past."

"Yes," agreed Elsa as she took the card and gave Deborah's hand a quick squeeze. "It's not what you hoped, but it's a good sign. I'll take this and put it with the other responses in your office. Mrs. Copeland told me to invite you to dinner tonight at Cumberland. Will you come?"

"Okay. I'll be there." Deborah led Elsa to the door. She no longer felt like cleaning. She decided the gardens needed a visit and went for a walk.

Deborah enjoyed dinner with those she considered her real family now. Catherine looked as regal as ever, but as benevolent as one could hope a queen might be, and Deborah could tell she loved having her family so close and so very happy. Simon was sober, and he and Denise were expecting twin boys. Copeland Park, the name they had chosen for their own estate, would soon be brimming with more joy than Simon had ever hoped for.

Oliver was doing very well. He and Sarah had made Cumberland their home, and Sarah was thriving. Away from Kelly Oliver was blooming. The submissiveness that had once defined Oliver was gone. In its place were happy confidence and freedom to enjoy being himself. He was going to counseling, working more and more, and taking control over his life. Catherine was careful not to give him orders or nag. She was extremely careful even in making suggestions, as she didn't want to replace his domineering and cruel ex-wife.

No one in the family had heard directly from Kelly. Her parents had sent a note to Sarah with a picture of Kelly on a beach with bright blue waters and simply said she was fine and missed Sarah. Sarah kept the photo under her pillow.

Mr. Song had other news, though. Kelly had married someone named Manuel Garcia. This gave Oliver the option of requesting child support for their daughter. Yet Oliver wanted nothing from her, nor did he need anything from her. To him, the marriage meant their ties were further cut.

It turned out Manuel Garcia was a sixty-six year old millionaire ex-pat living in Costa

Rica. Deborah prayed for the man. "Lord, protect him and give him a long life." She realized how facetious and judgmental she was being to assume that Kelly had married him for his money, or that she would harm him. That changed her perspective, so she tried to earnestly pray for Kelly and her new husband by adding to the prayer hopes for a happy marriage, and also salvation for both of them. She knew, however, she shouldn't assume that Kelly had married an older man, hoping he would not live long. Sixty-six years old was not elderly in today's world. He could very well have many years ahead of him. Deborah hoped so.

Knowing that Kelly was living in Costa Rica made Oliver nervous that she might suddenly want her daughter to visit, or worse yet, take custody. He couldn't bear to be the person responsible for separating a mother and child, though. So, instead of relinquishing her visitations, he had papers drawn up to ensure he would accompany Sarah out of the country for any visits, and that all visits regardless of where they took place would be supervised. It was sad, yet at the same time a relief, to know that Kelly would likely not fight this or bother with visitations. She had remained silent thus far, and a daughter would only interfere with her life in paradise. She had not bothered to even tell Sarah she was married. What would change so drastically?

That question made Deborah tremble with fear. She, Oliver, and Catherine decided together to simply give the question to God. They prayed together for Kelly and Manuel. They prayed for Sarah. At the end, they chose to trust the Lord with the situation.

Donna Campbell

THE WEDDING

WEDDING DAY

Deborah and Jackie walked across the lawn at Cumberland, where hours later the ceremony would take place. Workers lined chairs, and others followed behind covering the chairs with fabric. Two men were building the chuppah, which would soon be decorated with sunflowers, roses, and daisies to echo Deborah's bouquet. She watched as the chuppah took shape before her eyes, feeling as if she were overflowing with more joy than any person should have a right to experience.

Jackie said, "We might not have much chance after this, so I'd like to pray for you now, right here."

Deborah was already on the verge of happy tears and knew this would send her over the edge. "That sounds wonderful. Once I'm wearing my make-up, you may not say anything to make me cry."

"Please," said Jackie, "It doesn't take a word from me to make you cry. You're the best cryer I know." They hugged and laughed, then took hands and bowed their heads together. "Lord, our Maker, Daddy, as my sister and my friend stands tonight under your canopy, I ask that she will always remain under your protection. I pray that she and Ash will never leave you out of their marriage that the union will be the two of them together with you. Bless this event, but more so bless this marriage. I love this woman and I love the man you have chosen to be her husband. Give them more joy than they could hope for, bless them more than they can imagine, and make the two of them more than they can dream of being. Thank you. In Jesus' name, Amen."

Deborah was indeed crying by then, and Jackie slipped her a tissue. The two walked back to the house where Catherine, Denise, and Sarah would join them for spa treatments.

Deborah looked in the mirror and could barely believe she was looking at herself. She felt like a renaissance queen in her dress. Her dark hair was done up in an intricate style that she could never have done herself. Women flocked into the sitting room, which had been transformed for this time to congratulate Deborah. Jackie and Denise stayed by her side, and a photographer took photo after photo, occasionally asking the women to pose.

Deborah, Denise, and Jackie surprised the photographer when at one request for a pose they all made funny faces. Deborah laughed with the joy of who she had become and how far she had come since arriving in Belle Cay. There had been a time when anxiety made it impossible for her to let go and enjoy life. Now she didn't think twice about embracing happiness.

"Where is Catherine? I had hoped I might spend this time with her as well." Deborah kept waiting for her to arrive but she had not seen her since their hair and make-up had been done.

Denise answered too quickly. "I haven't seen her. I'm sure she's with Simon and Oliver somewhere."

"Well, I hope she comes soon." Deborah took her place in a chair centered in the room, with her friends surrounding her.

"I know she will," said Jackie.

Elana Arcola came into the room and offered her happy wishes. "Felicitations, dear Deborah. You are striking." She air-kissed each cheek and moved on to a tent outside for cocktails.

Finally Catherine entered the room. She stayed at the door at first. "Look at you! My sweet girl! Oh!"

"Thank you, Catherine." She began to stand to try and draw the woman inside but then saw who stood behind her and fell back into the chair.

Catherine stepped aside, and there stood Eileen Wade. "Deborah..." She stood quietly at the door.

Catherine took her by the hand and led her to her daughter. Catherine hugged Deborah tightly and whispered in her ear. "My gift for you today, one I hope will last forever."

Deborah tried not to cry. Jackie leaned in

close. "The make-up is waterproof. Let 'em flow." She handed her an entire box of tissues.

Deborah stood up and opened her arms to her mother. Eileen entered her embrace, and they said nothing for several minutes. Then it was Eileen who spoke.

"I know you never lied. Thank you for inviting me and giving me another chance. Being a guest at your wedding is more than I ever dreamed of for us. I know I'm not the mother you hoped for. I'm sorry."

Deborah couldn't think of her make-up now. Years' worth of tears poured down her face as she held her mother, and best of all, her mother held her. They eventually parted, and Deborah said, "Mom, I wonder if you might join Catherine in walking me down the aisle."

"Really? Oh, yes!"

Tears now flowed from every eye in the room. Even the photographer forgot to snap pictures for a few minutes.

While the women had their make-up reapplied, Deborah heard the story of how Eileen had come to be at the wedding. Elsa had shown the response to Catherine, who wasted no time in contacting Deborah's mother. It turned out that Eileen did want to attend and had legitimately not been able to afford the trip. Catherine had explained that she wanted this as a gift for Deborah. She paid for the entire trip and brought her to the Belle Cay hotel, arranging for everything.

"Catherine, I can't even imagine a better

gift," Deborah said. "Thank you." Then she turned to her mother. "Thank you too, Mom, for everything. I am so happy you're here. I've missed you."

Constance Deleon, who was applying Deborah's make-up for the second time that day, said, "Nope! No more tears just yet, ladies!" She swooped in to put the finishing touches on the bride's face.

ONE HAND ONE HEART

Deborah and Asher had planned a wedding that would integrate Jewish and Christian traditions. It would be something that fit them uniquely, using elements each liked from weddings they had read about or enjoyed. Deborah was once again in the sitting room, surrounded as before by many of the women who had already arrived. All spoke excitedly to one another, while Catherine and Eileen sat proudly on either side of her.

A loud shofar blast silenced the room for a moment. It was followed by another, and then the music and shouts of many men could be heard approaching the room. The joyfully dancing crowd entered the room. It was difficult to stay seated as Deborah searched the jubilant men for Ash. Finally the men parted and there he was, standing in front of her with shining dark curls. A huge smile spread across his face as he saw his bride. He approached, bent and gently lowered her veil across her face.

"It's time," he whispered. "It's finally time. I love you."

Deborah giggled with excitement and

whispered back. "I'm ready. I love you too."

Ash left the room with his parents and Jim Ramirez, by his side. He was followed by nearly everyone else to the lawn where the ceremony would take place. Once everyone had taken their places, the music began. Deborah, her mother, and Catherine watched the ceremony proceed as they waited for their cue.

Asher's parents walked him down the aisle to the spot where Allen Kennedy was standing. The Levines then lit a candle together and were led to their seats by Ash's band mates, Frank and Christian. Then it was time for Jim and Jackie to take their positions as the best man and maid of honor. Sarah followed behind, gathering flowers from the people seated at the edge of the aisle until she carried a bouquet of sunflowers, roses, and daisies.

The song changed to Wagner's "Bridal Chorus." Deborah's heart leaped with joy at the sound. She wanted to run down the aisle toward Asher, but walked instead with Catherine on one arm and her mother on the other. They brought her to Asher. Deborah took her bouquet from Sarah and walked around Asher seven times. He and she both silently mouthed the count together before she stood by his side. Eileen lit a candle, and the women were escorted to their seats by Simon and Oliver.

Now the couple stood together under the chuppah. Allen Kennedy gave a brief but moving speech about unity, love, and marriage. Deborah tried to listen carefully to his words and to take in every moment of the ceremony, but everything was a joyful blur. When the pastor at long last got to the vows, she was finally able to focus on the moment. She was one step closer to being Mrs. Levine. Sarah stepped up and took the flowers from Deborah.

Asher spoke first. "I take you, Deborah, to be my wedded wife. With deepest joy I receive you into my life that together we may be one. I promise to love you as Christ loves the church. I promise you my deepest love, my fullest devotion, my most tender care. I promise I will put God first and then you, honoring God's guidance by His Spirit through the Word of Jesus Christ. Therefore, throughout life, no matter what may lie ahead of us, I pledge to you my life as a loving and faithful husband and partner." He took a ring from his friend Brian and placed it on Deborah's finger.

Then it was Deborah's turn. She had expected to be nervous, but the nerves had melted away and all she could feel was bliss. "I take you, Asher, to be my wedded husband. With deepest joy I come into my new life with you. As you have pledged to me your life and love, so I too happily give you my life, and in confidence of your love submit myself to you as the church submits to Christ. I will put God first and then you, loving you and caring for you with my most tender affection. God has prepared me for you, and so I will ever strengthen, help, comfort, and encourage you. Therefore, throughout life, no matter what

Masquerade

may be ahead of us, I pledge to you my life as a faithful wife and partner." She took a ring from Dave and placed it on Ash's finger.

Allen Kennedy spoke. "As your first act as a married couple, you have requested to remember Jesus Christ by taking the Lord's Supper." He then offered them the bread and the wine representing Jesus' body and blood. The entire assembly prayed together. The pastor spoke about their inseparable union, but Deborah and Ash were looking at one another and not hearing much of what he said.

The small orchestra played "One Hand One Heart" by Leonard Bernstein as Ash and Deborah lit a long match from the candles on either side of them, and together lit the candle in front of them. Deborah's hands shook until Ash steadied them with his own.

Jim Ramirez took a glass carefully wrapped it in a white linen cloth and placed it at Ash's feet. Ash lifted his foot high and brought it down, smashing the glass to tiny shards. The crowd erupted with congratulatory cheers. When the noise had quieted, Allen spoke again. "This covenant with God and one another can never be broken, just as the fragments of this glass can never be put back together again. As Jesus has reconciled you to the Father through the Holy Spirit, and nothing can separate you from Him, we will one day unite with him perfectly forever. He has united the two of you to cling to one another and become one flesh. As He has united us with God, He has united

Deborah and Asher. They are no longer their own; they belong to one another as they belong to God. What God has made one, let no man separate. Asher, you may now kiss your bride."

Ash lifted Deborah's veil and kissed her softly. Music once more erupted from the small orchestra and Ash and Deborah walked down the aisle as husband and wife.

ONE SOUL

Most of Epsilon took the stage. As far as Deborah knew they were not supposed to play the wedding. Ash, though had a surprise for her. The band played a lovely melody. Ash took Deborah to the dance floor with a flair. The lights were low and a spot light shone on the bride and groom. Ash wrapped his arms around his beautiful wife. He began to sing, his clear voice coming through the sound system from a small microphone on his lapel.

One soul broken in two, plunged apart
(From God and each other)
One soul separated into two hearts
(Two halves looking for the other)

Love can't hide behind fancy words
Love isn't found in meaningless acts
One soul broken in two searched the world
One soul separated but wearing heavy masks

One soul broken in two, masks off
(Two halves of us)
One soul separated, Is that you my other

half
   (Three halves of us)

Love is seen, heard and known
Love was found in your sacrifice
One soul broken in two made one
One soul united for life

One soul united, masks off
(Two halves of us)
One soul made whole, Is that you my other half
   (Three halves of us)

Who am I without you?
I don't ever want to know.
Know me as I am
Know you as you are
Love me as I am meant to be
Love you as you're meant to be
Who am I? We are us.

All their friends and family applauded. Epsilon put their instruments down, and the wedding band picked up their own and played. Ash turned off his microphone and kissed his wife's forehead. Soon the dance floor was crowded with their friends and family. "You wrote me a song?" Deborah asked. "It's perfect." She didn't have the words to describe what it meant to her, so she embraced him and kissed him. "Are you determined to make me cry?"

Brian headed toward the couple and

handed Ash a rolled parchment. Without a word he was gone.

Ash gave the parchment to Deborah; he had written the lyrics out for her. "It's not the first one I wrote for you and it won't be the last. But this one is just for you. It's not an Epsilon song, it's your very own song."

"Aww! Sweetheart, I love it. I'm getting amazing gifts all around." They walked off the dance floor to their table and she read the lyrics over again, brimming with happiness. "You really are made for me."

"I'll be back soon," Ash told her. "I have something to do." He walked over to the table where Catherine, Eileen, and his mother and father were seated, then held his hand out to Eileen. "May I have this dance?"

Eileen blushed, but stood up and went to the dance floor with her son-in-law. "Are you a good man, Asher?" she asked.

"I hope I am," he answered earnestly. "I have to be, if I want to be with Deborah. She's the best person I've ever met. She has so much love to give. I want to give every bit and more back to her."

"I think you are. She deserves someone like you."

"I want you to know that you are welcome to be a part of this family. I mean, you are, but I want you to really be a part of it. If you want to live in Belleshore with us or near us, if you want to visit five times a year, I will do everything in my power to make that happen. I don't want you or Deborah to miss out on each other anymore, and I don't want to miss out on you. The past can be overcome, and you've done an amazing job so far. Please don't disappear from our lives again."

Eileen looked up at her tall son-in-law. "There's no chance you can get rid of me. I have a feeling I can find a dental hygienist job around here, and Catherine has already tried to tell me she knows of a lovely little guest cottage for rent somewhere close by.

"I happen to know a couple, newlyweds, Mr. and Mrs. Levine, who have an apartment in their house just for you, if you'll have them?"

"You barely know me. I'll tell you what. Let's all get to know each other, and that apartment can be my guestroom for now."

"Okay," he agreed with a smile as the song ended.

The DJ announced, "The groom's father has an announcement and a request." Michael Levine stepped up to the microphone. "I know Deborah thought she couldn't have a father/daughter dance tonight. But she is my daughter now." He looked at Deborah and the spotlight shone on her as she took a bite of chocolate cheesecake. "I would love the honor of dancing with you tonight." The band played "Just the Way You Are." Michael brought his daughter-in-law out to the dance floor.

This was one moment that Deborah had never thought she could experience. She felt as if everything she had lost over the years had been paid back to her a hundred times over.

Masquerade

Deborah and Ash made the rounds to table after table of people, all wishing them the best. She wanted to sit with each guest and talk, but there was no time. Even just including their very closest friends and relatives, taking Ash's large family and Deborah's growing one into consideration meant their "small" wedding had two hundred guests.

Deborah had been to no shortage of fun parties during her time in Belle Cay, and she knew she was biased, but her wedding party was the most fun out of all of them. Toast after toast rang out, wishing the couple happiness. Deborah looked around at her family. Nate danced with an enthralled Sarah. Katie and John chatted with Oliver in one corner, and Nya was flirting with Brian in another. The music played and the crowd danced. She watched as her friends and family celebrated life together. Eileen smiled up at Michael Levine as he danced with her until Ian cut in for a dance of his own. Michael then took his wife to the dance floor. Robert Song danced with Catherine. Simon danced with Jen as his very pregnant wife looked on. Deborah watched as Sarah chatted happily with her new "cousins," some of Ash's nieces, who Deborah realized were now her nieces as well.

Deborah was surrounded by the richness and joy of family, and all of it was hers. She held no fear that her dream would come crashing down around her. She had no worry that her happiness could be stolen. It was undying and never-ending gladness. It was love.

EPILOGUE

The church was filled to the brim. Ash and Deborah stood at the front of the sanctuary. Deborah held three-month-old Daniel in her arms, and Asher held the hand of Asha, the baby's three-year-old sister. Allen Kennedy stood beside them for the baby blessing ceremony.

"Asher and Deborah have served this church faithfully for the last several years. Deborah has been a leader for the teenaged girls among us. She has had more slumber parties and girls' days than Ash probably wants to remember. But he has been just as active in leading the youth of this church and lifting the music ministry to a level I didn't think was possible. Even as his professional band continues to reach new heights of success with their third album, Asher has been a faithful servant to God first, his family second, and this church third.

"I have heard many times, from the girls Deborah has spent time with, about the difference her compassion has made in their lives. I know of some who claim that it was Deborah's testimony that brought them to

Christ or even saved their lives. I've heard from all of the youth the love they have for Pastor Ash. Today, I have the pleasure of introducing this church to their second child, Daniel Evan Levine. They wish to ask all of you to join them in praying blessings over their son and their family. Will Deborah and Ash's family please come join us at the front as we lay hands on this family?"

It seemed as though half the congregation stood up and came to the front. Eileen Wade was first among them, and Asha leapt into her nana's arms. Michael and Eva approached, followed by Katy, her husband Carl, Nya, Nate, James, his wife Merri, John and his wife Leah, Jen and the rest of their grandchildren. Allen almost began speaking again, but Catherine, Oliver, Sarah, Simon, Denise and their four children also joined the family. Allen looked at the crowd and laughed. Once again he was about to begin speaking, but realized there were still more people coming up. Jackie, Ed and their three children were joined by Brian, Christian, Dave, and Frank, as well as each of their wives and all of their children. Next Jim and Andrea Ramirez and their two children joined the group.

Allen stood back and looked around the church with a smile. "Is there anyone else?" At last the rest of the congregation remained where they were. "Well, praise God. This is a big and beautiful family you have here. These children, all of them, are in good hands. Let's pray.

"Father, thank you for this family, for

these people who love them dearly. Bless this child, hold him in your hands, and lead him along your path. Let each of us in this family and in this church step up and do what is right for this little boy, his sister, and his parents. He is yours and we are yours. In Jesus' name, Amen."

As Deborah carried Daniel back to their seats, her mind began drifting back several years, settling on her initial arrival at Cumberland all those years before. She had come to Connecticut alone, convinced she would always be alone; she'd had no family, and thought she never would. She began to laugh in spite of herself. If God had given her then a sneak peek of what her life was like now – carrying a child, with another in tow, a wedding ring on her hand, and her mother smiling over at her – she simply would not have believed Him.

Yet He had never given up on her. No matter how she ignored Him, no matter how she made terrible choices, He kept right on pursuing her, until she finally accepted and let Him put her in the place where she was more satisfied than she had ever dreamed possible.

Ash noticed the huge smile on her face. "What are you so happy about?" he asked.

"Everything," she answered contentedly. Placing her spare arm around her husband, she knew the hope of her present and her future was in her heart and in her hands. More than that it was in God's hands. What reason was there not to be filled with joy?

Masquerade

ABOUT THE AUTHOR

Donna is an ordained minister, author, and blogger living in Ocoee, Florida. She remains active as she works toward a master's degree in Christian counseling, writing the daily devotional blog Salt & Light and serving God through street and prayer ministries with The Church of Life in Orlando, Florida's tourist district. You can read her blogs at www.DonnaLCampbell.com and check out the church at www.TheChurchofLife.com Follow Donna on Facebook at www.facebook.com/DonnaCampbellBooks and
www.facebook.com/SaltnLightBibleBlog

Printed in Great Britain
by Amazon